DOMAIN

< < ROHAN GAVIN > >

INK ROAD

First published in the UK in 2025 by
INK ROAD
an imprint of Bonnier Books UK
5th Floor, HYLO, 105 Bunhill Row, London EC1Y 8LZ

Copyright © Rohan Gavin 2025

All rights reserved.
No part of this publication may be reproduced, stored or transmitted
in any form or by any means, electronic, mechanical, photocopying or
otherwise, without the prior written permission of the publisher.

The right of Rohan Gavin to be identified as Author of this work has
been asserted by him in accordance with the Copyright, Designs and
Patents Act, 1988.

This is a work of fiction. Names, places, events and incidents are either
the products of the author's imagination or used fictitiously.
Any resemblance to actual persons, living or dead, or actual
events is purely coincidental.

A CIP catalogue record for this book is available from the British Library.

ISBN: 978-1-78530-798-0

1 3 5 7 9 10 8 6 4 2

Typeset by Data Connection
Printed and bound in Great Britain by Clays Ltd, Elcograf S.p.A.

The authorised representative in the EEA is
Bonnier Books UK (Ireland) Limited.
Registered office address: Floor 3, Block 3,
Miesian Plaza, Dublin 2, D02 Y754, Ireland
compliance@bonnierbooks.ie

bonnierbooks.co.uk/InkRoad

For Stanley. I started writing this for you but couldn't have finished it without you!

In 2004, Japanese scientists at Nippon Telephone & Telegraph discovered that the body's electric field could be used to transmit and receive data at broadband speeds. (*Source: MIT Technology Review*)

CHAPTER ONE
Flight 39

If the plane got into trouble at over thirteen thousand feet, the cabin could lose pressure, spelling catastrophe. It was a simple matter of bend ratios and breaking points, cause and effect. Only three people on board the flight from New York's JFK to Los Angeles knew this: the two airline pilots with their combined three thousand hours of training, and the teenage boy with dark hair and dark clothes seated in 24D – listed on the passenger manifest as SIMMS, PORTER. Though exactly *how* he knew this wasn't all that easy to explain.

Despite having wisdom beyond his years, there were many things Porter didn't know, like why someone had targeted the airliner, or how this act of sabotage would be carried out. Maybe his boss didn't know herself. Or maybe she did, and she'd chosen not to tell him. After all, she'd only informed him of the threat *after* take-off, once the plane was airborne. *Very helpful*, he thought.

In any case, at the rate they were climbing, the desired altitude would soon be reached, and the question fatefully answered.

Meanwhile, the other passengers carried on watching their screens, sharing light conversation about final destinations, hopes and dreams, oblivious to the dark plans that were running like code in the background of their everyday reality, determining the event that was about to happen.

As if on cue, the plane banked sharply and an alarm bleated through the cabin, causing concerned yelps that quickly became screams. A moment later, the cries were muted when plastic panels flipped open overhead, dropping a shower of oxygen masks dangling from lengths of rubber tubing, swaying as gravity was challenged. The masks were snatched and hurriedly strapped on.

The plane rolled hard in the opposite direction, then seemed to yaw in a lazy circle, with the sickening glee of a roller-coaster ride. Unsecured items, bags, laptops and other devices, anything that wasn't tied down, took flight, sticking to the ceiling.

Amidst the chaos, for a split second, Porter thought again about his harsh boss, and her equally harsh daughter – and if he'd ever see the unusual girl again, or any other living soul for that matter. Then he reminded himself to push any irrelevant thoughts to the wall, confining them to the outer chambers of his mind to make way for cold, hard logic. The passengers tightened their seat belts, adjusted their oxygen masks and held on to their armrests for dear life. Porter did the opposite, unbelted and slid out from his seat, staggering up the tilting craft like he was climbing a flight of stairs.

A flight attendant leaned out of her jump seat and attempted to wave him back down the aisle, then her head suddenly lolled as she slouched in her chair. It must have been the masks. Perhaps there was too much oxygen being fed to them: that would cause drowsiness. He knew this from climbing mountains back home.

Porter glanced behind him to see the rest of the passengers all sitting neatly in rows, frozen in time: asleep. He turned back, taking two more thudding strides to reach out and hammer on the cockpit door, but before he could do so, it opened by itself, as he was met by the masked co-pilot, who promptly fell headlong to the cabin floor, unconscious.

Porter grabbed hold of the door to steady himself, stepped over the smartly uniformed body and entered the cockpit to find a male pilot and female crew member slumped at their posts, with the night sky beyond. The joystick that was supposed to be controlling the craft was moving by itself, as if possessed, sending the plane into another uncontrolled roll – then pitching forward into a dive. The jet engines wailed in complaint. Porter hauled the pilot aside and took his seat at the flightdeck, strapping himself in, his black jacket and jeans at odds with the uniformed crew sprawled unconscious around him. He closed his eyes for a moment and focused on what he had to do.

Frantic chatter from the control tower interrupted him. A man's urgent voice repeating: 'I say again, Flight 39 . . . maintain altitude. Do you read?'

Porter picked up the headset, adjusted the size and put it on, keeping a calm tone: 'Mayday, mayday, this is flight three-niner, declaring an emergency, request permission to land.'

'Wait . . . Who is this?'

'That doesn't matter.'

'How old are you?'

'That doesn't matter either.'

Porter blinked:

Searching . . .

His eyes still closed, he answered, 'The plane's been compromised. One hundred and five souls on board. Disengaging autopilot and moving to hands-on.' Porter opened his eyes, moving his hands over the controls, pressing a series of buttons and switches.

'Wait, what? You can't fly that plane!'

'Yes I can.'

He blinked again:

Connecting . . .

'Request vectors to departure airport,' Porter muttered. 'Roll equipment for landing.'

A pause, then the control tower answered, begrudging. 'Roger that . . . whoever this is. Standby for vectors.'

Porter exhaled and hauled back on the joystick, coasting through an opening in the clouds and levelling out into a controlled descent. The cockpit gauges rebalanced themselves. Neon light burst through the grey strata, revealing a tidy grid of rooftops and tree crowns spanning the suburbs below. The cockpit fell silent over the drone of the engines. Porter steadied his breathing, then a sharp pain jolted his head, until he blinked it away.

'Flight three-niner, you're cleared to land,' the controller's voice rattled.

The airliner rocked, buffeted by a strong wind as Porter gripped the stick with both hands and performed a wide circle, setting a return course for New York.

CHAPTER TWO
The Long Way Home

The plane landed without incident at JFK Airport on a specially cleared runway swarming with emergency vehicles. After bringing the aircraft to a full stop, Porter left the cockpit and walked briskly past the rows of unconscious travellers: kids, parents, whole families with their heads resting on each other's shoulders. He retook his seat, 24D, turned up the collar of his jacket to deflect the chill of the air conditioning, then pretended to be asleep, waiting to be woken by the authorities, along with the others. The headache made playing unconscious easy. Through his closed lids, he heard the metallic sounds of jet bridges connecting to the fuselage, and it triggered something deep inside his head – an image, half-seen, dreamlike:

<< Snow and ice thud against the underside of a Cadillac SUV. A driver in a chauffeur's hat navigates a blizzard, cleared once per second by the windscreen wipers.

'Shouldn't be much longer 'til we rejoin the 33,' the driver announces.

Porter is younger, sunk in the backseat, glancing between a well-dressed, forty-something white man and his Indian wife, beaming down at him: his parents. They exchange a smile, but Porter's focus is elsewhere: a wire descends from his bobble hat, connected to a screen balanced on his lap, showing a chessboard with icons of kings, queens and knights.

'Hasn't he had enough screen time?' his mother asks her husband, who's hunkered over a laptop, his eyes smart and tenacious, while hers are warmer, more understanding. Both have English accents.

'Not yet - he's about to beat me,' the dad replies, his laptop screen split between the chessboard and a dashboard of readouts, under a crest that reads:

Department Of Machine and Artificial INtelligence

Porter uses his finger to move the knight across the chequerboard screen, toppling his opponent's king.

'Checkmate. You did it, Porter!' his dad calls out, removing the wire from under his son's hat.

'That's ... impossible,' says his mother. 'He's five, and you're–'

At that moment, another vehicle rear-ends theirs, pushing the SUV across the ice like a child's toy. Twin sets of blazing headlights light up the cabin from the front-end of an even bigger four-wheel drive, right behind them.

'What's happening?' cries his mother.

The vehicle behind them accelerates again, performing a 'PIT' manoeuvre, nudging the SUV towards a steep snowbank. The SUV slides, rotating gracefully, before slamming into the icy shoulder of the road.

The hiss of the engine fogs up the windscreen; the driver is unconscious at the wheel. Porter's dad kicks open the rear passenger door, physically dragging his wife and son out of the cabin, using the wreckage as cover. Pennsylvania's Pocono Mountains are just visible through the snowstorm.

The enemy vehicle waits at a distance, lights glaring, engine revving, exhausts pluming on either side of the huge chassis. Porter's dad looks at it, apprehensive, then back to his son, shivering under his mother's arm.

'We're going to play a different game,' he tells him.

Porter's pale grey eyes search the snowy wastes, finding no identifying signs, nowhere to hide or seek. It is the featureless landscape of a dream. 'Why?'

'Do as your father says.' His mother smothers him in a hug.

His dad kneels. 'I want you to run and hide in that outcrop of trees over there. We'll find you.' He points to a dim shape above the snowbank, some two hundred metres away, signposted by an intoxicating pine smell. 'Run as fast as you can and don't look back. That's how you win. Okay?'

'Okay,' Porter answers.

His mother and father clutch him in an embrace, then hoist him up on the snowbank and let him go, slipping across the drift, obediently scrambling off into the white-out.

Porter runs, confused, but grinning at the prospect of hiding from his parents and surprising them with a terrifying yell. The trees ahead of him take shape in the haze, but they don't look inviting. He turns from the shelter of the treeline to check on his parents. Instead, he sees a series of scattered shapes through the blizzard; nothing that he can piece together into a picture that makes any sense. His face drops, unsure if this is part of the game.

'Are you coming or not . . . ?' he calls. To his surprise, there's no reply, just the howl of the snow churning into a vortex.

Then three figures emerge from the mist, dressed in black, fanning out across the field, as if searching for him – though none of them resemble his parents, and none appear friendly. Confused, Porter backs away, nearly tripping up as he retreats into the woods, locating a trunk to hide behind.

Suddenly, a gloved hand clamps over Porter's mouth and his entire body is pulled backwards through the snow, behind the treeline, out of sight. Trying to scream, he looks up to examine his captor: a man of similar age to his father, but speckled with leaves and pines, his face unshaven but kind, under the brim of a wool hunting hat, an old rifle slung over his oilskin jacket. He doesn't smell like his father; he smells of earth.

'It's okay, I won't hurt you,' the man whispers. 'My name's Joe,' he adds.

Porter yelps and claws at the man's arm, but his hands slip on the oilskin. After a few minutes, exhausted, Porter stops fighting and sinks into the creased, leather collar. Images of kings and knights and rooks flash through his mind, but he can't tell which one this man represents.

The hunter removes his jacket and wraps it around the boy, then angles his rifle scope from the darkness of the woods, watching through the scratched crosshairs as the three sinister figures approach through the snow at twenty metres apart. They touch their ears, as if in communication with each other, or someone else, before turning back in the direction of the wrecked SUV that Porter was travelling in. One of the figures is caught by the wind, his jacket opening to reveal a glimpse of a shield. Joe mouths the letters silently. 'F ... B ... I ...' Returning to the crash site, the figures unroll two black body bags and lay them out on the ground. The hunter observes, his jaw agape.

'Can't tell ... Can't tell anyone,' Joe mutters to himself, then picks up Porter and jolts further uphill into the woods, using a tree branch to cover his tracks. >>

'Wake up, son.' An emergency worker in a yellow jacket woke Porter from his dreamlike memory, then moved on to the next row of seats, working his way up the aisle. Porter wiped beads of sweat from his brow and joined the others.

One by one, the passengers were roused, disoriented, reaching for their hand luggage, before being guided through the aircraft door to the jet bridge. While the travellers were ferried to a lounge in the terminal building for trauma counselling, Porter separated from the group, slipping through a set of glass screens and into the arrivals area.

Raising his eyes to the upper corner of his vision, he asked no one in particular: 'Where's the car?'

Receiving an answer, he nodded and walked to the red zone outside the terminal where a black SUV was waiting for him. He opened the rear passenger door and hopped inside.

Twenty minutes later, the SUV pulled up at the kerb of a brownstone townhouse on a quiet Manhattan street lined with London plane trees. On stepping out of the car, Porter noticed a light on in an upstairs window that was normally dark. He paused, then jogged up the steps to the front door, which opened to receive him.

His boss Mallory's form filled the doorway: African American, around fifty, spry but solidly built with short, clipped hair contrasted by her oversized spectacles. The orange glow of the fireplace flickered behind her, as if she was some kind of gatekeeper.

'Bumpy landing?' she asked in her Southern lilt. He ignored the quip and walked past her into the entrance hall. 'Congratulations,' she said after him.

'Do I get to know who I saved?'

'Every soul on board. The rest is "need to know".'

'Can we cut the cloak and dagger stuff?' he asked.

'Sometimes circumstances require us to wear a cloak and carry a dagger.'

Porter rubbed his temples, impatient with her games. 'You might want to know I had another flashback. It was more intense this time. It sort of feels like I might be losing my mind.'

She closed the front door and turned to face him, as impressive as she was when they'd first met. That felt like a lifetime ago, even though it was just over a week.

'It's called Random Access Memory,' she reminded him. 'What you're describing is a normal side effect.'

'You told me the side effects were mild.'

'The mind is a complex device.'

'I don't like being referred to as a device,' Porter's voice rose.

Mallory glanced up the staircase and lowered her own voice. 'Maud's back from Andover for the weekend – her journey was almost as taxing as yours.'

Porter doubted that. He noted a wheelie bag and school satchel at the foot of the stairs and the sound of distant music from an upper floor. The girl was upstairs, and the thought of it was almost as terrifying as the ride he'd just been on.

'She's tired and needs to rest,' Mallory warned.

Porter caught a glimpse of socked feet behind the railings at the top of the staircase, then looked back, pretending he hadn't noticed.

'As you know,' his boss carried on, 'my daughter knows nothing of our work. . . and that is how it will stay.'

'I know the rules.'

Porter climbed the stairs to the landing, then continued to the spare room that had become his temporary home. From the end of the corridor, beyond his quarters, distorted indie music reverberated from a vinyl record player, like a siren calling him. He followed the sound to a door hanging ajar.

Behind it were exposed wooden floors, a single sconce light, a ballet barre and a mirror taking up one wall. Holding on to the barre was Mallory's teenage daughter, in sweats and socks, perfectly poised, one leg extended, staring at the mirror. Porter realised she wasn't watching herself; instead she was looking directly at his reflection.

'Hi . . .' he managed.

She had the same expression she'd had the first time he saw her: lips slightly parted in perpetual amusement, dark skin and braids framing wide green eyes that were almost too wide for her face.

'Still here?' she asked.

'I guess.'

'Even if your mind's elsewhere.'

'I don't know what you mean.'

'Yes, you do,' she answered. 'I'm not as clueless as I appear.' Footsteps approached across the landing. 'We can't talk any more—'

Mallory's voice interrupted them: 'Darling . . . ?' Her imposing figure appeared behind them in the doorway. 'Porter was just going to his room.'

'Good,' Maud responded. 'He was bothering me.'

Porter's face blushed as he withdrew from the doorway. Maud returned to her exercises, swivelled her hips, extended her foot and gave the door a soft kick, tilting her chin and looking into the mirror, betraying a smile as the door swung closed, blocking him out.

CHAPTER THREE
The Proposition

That evening, Porter heard sharp voices from downstairs, muffled by the thick, crimson-carpeted floors. A loud slam heralded silence, followed a moment later by the march of footsteps and the creak of his bedroom door opening. Mallory's silhouette appeared in the doorway.

Porter looked up from the book he was pretending to read. 'Is everything okay?' he asked.

His boss stood backlit by the glow of the landing. 'Sometimes Maud has difficulty with . . . boundaries. You don't need to concern yourself with our affairs. It will only serve as a distraction.'

Porter tossed the book aside. 'It's human nature to be curious. I am still human, remember?'

Mallory stepped forward, filling the space, her presence less maternal than threatening. 'Need I remind you: we're not family. I'm the teacher and you're here to learn. And my daughter, and anything that comes out of her pretty little mouth, is not to be relied upon – do we understand each other?'

Porter ignored the slur and carried on. 'Here to learn what exactly?'

'How to focus, to deploy your abilities to their most positive effect. The way your parents envisaged.'

'I hardly remember them – that's the problem,' Porter replied.

'The brain recalls what it needs to – *when* it needs to,' she added with a sphinx-like nod. 'Now get some rest,' she ordered, closing the door behind her.

That night, when sleep came, his half-remembered vision returned:

<< At fourteen, Porter overtakes Joe, knowing the mountain paths almost better than his surrogate parent does. He also carries a heavier pack and matching rifle, hopping over rocks and tree stumps, not unlike the animal they are currently tracking.

'Take a breath. Let's check our bearings,' Joe sighs, leaning on a sheer cliff face, more for his own benefit than map-reading purposes.

They are high up now, where the air is thin, and funnels of vapour seem to defy gravity, gliding up from the chasms below.

'Why do we always stop here?' Porter had wanted to ask this a thousand times, but was afraid that by scratching the surface of their backcountry life he might cause it to crumble and fall apart.

'Creature of habit, I guess,' Joe replies with a shrug, but Porter could always tell when he was holding something back. The hunter gazes under a sheet of cloud at the landscape below, recalling the events when this unusual kid had been left with him.

'That's where it happened, isn't it?' says Porter.

'I don't know what happened,' Joe answers. 'It was a hit-and-run in zero visibility.'

Porter recalls the story Joe told him when he turned ten; how the driver hadn't stopped; how the authorities couldn't be trusted; 'But you can rely on me ... I'll keep you safe,' Joe had assured him.

Porter spent every night tallying it with his own memories: the backseat of the SUV, sitting huddled between his parents, the blizzard, the shapes in the snow. Images, once so vivid, that had worn thin with time and were now as vague as figures observed through frosted glass, that couldn't be grasped, only grabbed at. Still, the pain of losing his parents was a burden on Porter's mind, carrying with it anxiety, a sort of weightless feeling, adrift without answers, and an anger that he kept buried but he suspected would one day break out like a zombie and stalk the earth. God help whoever had taken them from him.

'Whoever was responsible,' Joe says, as if reading his mind, 'there's no point trying to settle the score. The best revenge is to live your life, do something good with it.' He raises a hand, hearing something upwind of them, then crouches against the cliff face.

Porter follows suit, training his rifle over a stone plateau into the shade of a pine tree some three hundred metres away. The antlers, then the head of the deer emerge from behind a boulder: a male – a buck – its bold profile presenting the perfect target, framed by pinecones.

'Take the shot ...' Joe whispers.

Porter levels the crosshairs of the sight; then gently squeezes the trigger, until, at the last moment, he raises the barrel an inch and fires. The crack of the gunshot echoes through the mountains – sparing the deer, which turns tail and bolts. A pinecone drops in its place.

Joe pats him on the shoulder to console him. 'Ten to one I woulda missed it myself.'

Porter raises his rifle again, tucking it under his armpit, squeezing off two more shots, unblinking.

Joe watches as two pinecones explode and fall to the ground. 'Better ...'

'Thanks.'

'Better get back and do your homework.'

Joe's Ford Bronco winds down the mountain, finally pulling up at a modest wood-framed house in the village of Tannersville, at the foot of the Poconos. Through the windshield, a vehicle blocks the driveway: a black-tinted station wagon. They have visitors. The doors open to unload an odd couple: a thin, older man in a grey suit, and a broadly built African-American woman around fifty, with clipped hair and oversized spectacles.

'Help you with somethin'?' Joe calls out to them, stepping down from his truck, keeping one hand on the driver's seat - resting on his rifle.

His girlfriend, Sally, forty with bookish glasses, appears on the stoop, not expecting guests.

The grey suit approaches Joe with his hands meekly raised, to indicate they mean no harm. Then he takes a business card from his top pocket and holds it out. Joe squints at the print. 'I ... S ... S?' he asks, perplexed.

'International Social Service.'

'Meaning?' says Joe.

The woman has joined Sally on the stoop, where she delivers a warm smile, accompanied by a Southern lilt: 'Excuse Mr Wexel. He can get a little hung up on abbreviations. It means caring for the vulnerable. Connecting children with their parents. That type of thing.'

'If you'd like to leave some information,' Sally offers, 'we'd be happy to make a donation.'

'That won't be necessary,' the woman politely rebuffs her. 'But we'd like to give you some information. My name is Mallory Munroe.' She extends a hand to Joe. 'I believe yours is Joseph O'Neill.' Then she turns to Porter, who leans his rifle on his hip. 'And you must be ...?'

'Trouble if you come any closer.'

'Nice to meet you, Porter,' Mallory replies, unfazed. 'I was a friend of your parents ... Mind if I come in?'

Porter freezes. Sally's good manners get the better of her and she ushers the pair into the house, as Elvis sings 'Can't Help Falling In Love' from an old turntable. The walls are covered in photos of Porter and Joe on various adventures, hikes and outdoor pursuits. A coffee table is strewn with fantasy novels, tech magazines and half-completed homework. Mallory takes it in without expression. She seems too imposing for the confines of the house - too worldly.

'Can I get you some coffee?' Sally asks.

'Bless your heart.'

Joe gives his partner a disapproving look, then turns to their uninvited guest. 'What's all this about?'

'It took us a while to find you,' Mallory says with grudging respect.

Porter answers, 'If you came to do a welfare check, to check I'm happy here, well, I am. One hundred percent.' Something catches in his voice, betraying his words - not because he didn't love Joe and Sally as the only parents he could remember, but because, despite their best efforts, he knows this isn't where he's meant to be. It's a connecting stop to somewhere else.

Mallory takes a seat at the dining table, spreading her hands, as if giving a presentation. 'Your parents were colleagues of mine: Professor Connor and Doctor Aayra Simms.'

'Connor and Aayra,' Porter repeats like a sermon.

'That's right. They were also my friends.' She pushes a Polaroid photo across the table, showing a handsome, mixed-race couple that Porter instantly recognises as his parents. The photo confirms what Porter already suspected: that they'd left him with broader shoulders, darker hair and an olive complexion – unlike Joe and Sally's.

'They were scientists,' Mallory goes on. 'Connor was born and raised in London, Aayra in Mumbai. They met at college, then were drafted to work in a department of the US government that deals with technology.'

'What type of technology?' Porter asks.

Mallory takes something out of her pocket: a small, scorched cable with two rusted electrodes attached to the end of it. 'This was recovered from the wreckage. We think you could help us figure out what it is.'

Porter stops, arrested by the sight of the damaged gadget in the palm of her hand: the memories flooding back; and, with them, suspicion.

'I've never seen it before in my life,' he lies.

Mallory judges her next move carefully, sliding a business card across the table. It has 'NY, NY' printed on it. 'When you're ready ... be in touch.'

'What happened in the snow?' Porter demands.

'An accident. The other driver failed to stop; weather hampered the inquiry.' She looks to Joe. 'Mr O'Neill never contacted the authorities. If he witnessed something, that's a question for his conscience.'

Joe bursts out, 'Don't listen to them, Porter. For all we know, this is a pack of lies ...'

Mallory snaps back, 'Lies? You think you can keep him here forever? One day somebody's going to figure out that he's not your sister's boy. That you don't even have a sister.'

Joe swallows hard.

'If you come with us,' she tells Porter, tapping the business card, 'I can tell you about your parents ... about their work.'

Sally stands next to Joe for support, their fingers interlinking until they go white.

'You'll be compensated for your loss,' Wexel adds.

'We don't want your money,' Sally fires back.

Porter stays focused on the stranger. 'The answer's no.'

Mallory nods. 'We'll show ourselves out.'

Porter watches from his bedroom window as the odd couple return to the station wagon and start the engine. Then the tinted rear window rolls down to reveal a girl's face in the backseat. She is around his age, with dark skin, braided hair tied back, framing wide green eyes - almost too wide for her face, her lips slightly parted in perpetual amusement. Porter observes, mesmerised. She looks upwards, staring right at him. Ashamed, he withdraws, leaving a circle of moisture on the glass, which causes her to smile triumphantly as the car window rolls up, obscuring her slender neck and straight nose, leaving only a glimpse before she is blocked out completely. >>

CHAPTER FOUR
Activation

Porter woke in a cold sweat. The house felt quieter than usual. He swung his legs out of bed, put on some clothes, then padded down the corridor to Maud's room, but the door was strangely ajar, and the ballet barre deserted.

When he reached the kitchen, he found Mallory at the stove, frying eggs and hash browns with the brutal efficiency of a short order cook.

'Where's Maud?' he asked.

'Like I said, that's not your concern.' Mallory flipped the eggs.

Porter sat down at the kitchen table, and she slid a breakfast plate towards him, concluding the exchange, then shuffled off her apron to reveal a garish tweed ensemble, at odds with Porter's T-shirt and sweats.

'Eat up,' she ordered. 'We have work to do.'

After breakfast, he followed her to the study that was lined on every side by mahogany bookcases. She reclined in a dark leather wingback chair leaving him to take the uncomfortable wooden desk opposite.

'Is this what my parents wanted for me? To study alone, in a jail cell?'

'You're never technically alone, remember?'

'That's what worries me. What's inside my head.'

'The brain is a peculiar thing. It's still the most powerful processor on Earth. It is the singular lens through which we view the world. Many believe it defines reality . . . that there is no reality except what we perceive with our own mind.'

'I know. I've seen *The Matrix*.'

She ignored him and carried on. 'As you know, your parents' obsession was unlocking the potential of the mind. To bring information to our fingertips. Of course, smartphones already do that. They're the closest to superpowers that we have; they expand our knowledge base, tell us where we are, where to go, how to do things; they grant us access to almost anything, 24/7. The challenge was to harness that power without the use of a physical device. Just the human brain.'

'I get it. Some entrepreneurs tested it on monkeys. You chose me.'

'If you remember, we didn't have another option.'

'How could I forget?'

<< Mallory sits in the same room some days earlier, in the same wingback chair, lecturing Porter, his checked hunting jacket discarded on a nearby sofa.

'You did the right thing coming here.'

The scorched cable and electrodes retrieved from his parents' car wreck are visible on a side table.

'You didn't leave me much choice,' he answers.

'Joe and Sally will understand.'

'I'm here because you promised me the truth about my real parents.'

'Okay,' she replies. 'Then we'll begin.' She sits back in her seat. 'We've known for some time that the body's electromagnetic field can be used to send and receive data.'

'You mean like Wi-Fi?' asks Porter.

'Exactly. Data can be streamed from a central server, through a specially designed interface, direct to the brain - the frontal lobe to be exact, where short-term memories are stored. Like RAM.'

'Random Access Memory,' Porter responds.

Mallory nods. 'In a regular human brain, the frontal lobe stores six to eight memories, for quick retrieval. In an enhanced brain ... it could be ten to fifteen times that.'

Porter feels like he's in science class, only this time he suspects the specimen is him. 'What is the interface?' he asks.

'Good question. In early prototypes it was this ...' She refers to the charred electrodes from the car crash. 'Then, we experimented with neural implants: a microchip embedded in the brain tissue. But it attracted too much attention: media, animal and human rights activists - all genuine concerns, of course. Besides, it wasn't effective. It caused other issues ...' She trails off, leaving the impression that the experiment had not been a success. 'The breakthrough came when we realised that positively and negatively charged nanoparticles could be used to generate electrical impulses in the neural pathways. To generate virtual memories and new abilities ... sort of like apps.'

'Apps?' Porter's powers of concentration fail him.

She smiles. 'Don't worry, I'll show you.'

Now downtown, Porter enters the lobby of a modern skyscraper, flanked by Mallory and Wexel. They enter a mirrored elevator and the floor numbers start ticking upwards.

'The nanoparticles are introduced nasally - as a spray,' Mallory explains. 'They act as microconductors to livestream data to your brain. No fiddly implants or electrodes. The particles stay active in your system for around twenty-four hours.'

'What kind of data can be streamed?'

'Almost anything. We discovered younger people with younger brains performed better. They were able to absorb the information more easily. We believe this is due to the accelerated learning curve of the growing mind. They were also able to readily communicate that information through the spinal cord to the rest of the body, adopting abilities they never previously had.'

'Like what?'

'Practically anything, from the chess you played with your parents as a child, to advanced math, to fighting skills.' She pauses. 'Your parents called it "channelling".'

'Hhn,' says Porter, a little spooked, turning the idea over in his mind. She was describing what amounted to the world's greatest video game, but they weren't talking about virtual reality. This was real life. 'I'm sure you can find smarter, fitter kids than me.'

'We ran trials on several candidates before we realised: when your parents created the technology, they tailored the software to the best person available to them.'

Porter points his finger at his own head. She nods.

'So I'm your only shot,' he says.

'It would appear that way.'

The elevator doors sweep open and Porter follows Mallory and Wexel along a glass corridor, some thirty floors above New York City.

'How d'you know it'll work?' he asks.

'We don't. Yet. We're hoping you'll agree to a trial run.'

'Not until I know what it's gonna be used for.'

'You're smart, Porter, figure it out. The applications are endless. What if national security was at stake? What if lives were in danger? What if it was hundreds of lives, or thousands? Would that change your mind?'

'You're talking apps, numbers. Zeros and ones,' he goes on. 'If you want my help, you need to put it in a language I can understand.'

'Life versus death. Is that clear enough?'

Wexel guides Porter and Mallory into a sparse reception room where a twenty-something woman in natty, blue-rimmed spectacles reclines with a laptop, her sneakers propped on the desk – then, registering their arrival, springs from her chair to open an adjacent door. It leads to a dark chamber, lined with racks of whirring hardware and strobing lights, ventilated by rows of fans. Holding the laptop under her arm, the young woman opens a further door, which gives on to a black abyss.

Something clicks, and the room illuminates to reveal four giant white walls, so seamless and opaque that its true dimensions cannot be determined. The only reference point is the presence of two clinical-looking plastic bucket chairs and a small, steel medical table on wheels occupying one corner of the space.

'This is Adriane,' Mallory begins.

The young woman bows a little. 'You can call me Ade,' she says. 'Like First Aid. Should be easy to remember, seeing as that's sort of my job.'

Porter looks confused.

'Ade is a programmer,' Mallory spells it out.

'Programming what exactly?' Porter asks.

'Well, basically ... you,' says Ade.

Porter examines the white walls, then the floor that is only lightly scuffed, due to what he assumes are Ade's sneakers. The tread marks lead off into the distance like the tracks of a lone survivor on a desert island.

'Don't worry,' says Ade, 'all will become clear.'

'Take a seat and we'll get started,' suggests Mallory, gesturing to one of the plastic chairs by the steel instrument table. On the surface of the table is a slim, nylon case, which she unfastens to reveal a short, silver cylinder.

'What's that?' asks Porter.

'I'm sure you've seen one of these before.' Mallory pops the cap off the cylinder to reveal a pointed spray head. 'Like when you have a cold?' She sprays an innocent mist into the air between them.

Porter eyes the device with suspicion. 'I've never seen one like that before. I think I might want a doctor's note. No offence, but neither of you look much like doctors.'

Mallory takes a seat, encouraging Porter to join her. 'As we discussed, the digital interface is created by a fine mist of nanoparticles that line the nasal passages, pass through the olfactory nerve - where we get our sense of smell - and, from there, travel directly to the brain—'

Porter stops her. 'We discussed the theory, not the practice.'

Mallory nods. 'A theory your parents dreamed up - at great taxpayer expense, I might add. Close to a billion dollars in today's money. And it will remain a theory unless you agree to the trial.' She holds his stare with a tight smile. 'Unless of course you'd prefer to return to Tannersville. We can arrange that too.' There was no sense of threat, just the quiet confidence of someone who had already calculated every move.

Ade shifts in her sneakers, preferring to stick to the science. 'The particles act as microconductors, switching the neural pathways of the brain on and off.' She uses her thumb and forefinger to make a clicking motion in the air. 'Like a light switch. Similar to the way resistors work in a silicon chip.'

'And the data is transmitted via my body's electric field? From … a cloud?'

'Top of the class. The cloud server is where I do my work. The data is managed by us, then sent to you … the domain.'

'So I'm not a person any more? I'm a www-dot … ?'

Ade smiles. 'I'll admit, we did nickname you Porter.com - for trial purposes only. It's a little on the nose.'

Porter's eyes return to the nasal spray. 'And the particles stay active for twenty-four hours?'

Ade pauses. 'According to tests on humanised mice.'

'That's reassuring.'

'We think so,' says Ade, not registering his sarcasm.

'I think that's enough science class for now.' Mallory slides the silver cylinder towards Porter, who watches it rock and glimmer on the table under the room's flat white light. Wexel appears at his shoulder, cradling an iPad, its screen open on a legal document, covered in yellow, highlighted signature lines.

'Tap here, here ... here ...' Wexel orders, waiting for Porter to place his finger on the glass.

Porter looks around the white, featureless room, then back to the iPad screen. 'I guess there's no point reading the Ts and Cs?'

'Not really,' Wexel replies. 'We're in uncharted waters. The only people who knew more about the technology than us were your parents. And they're gone obviously,' he says without emotion.

Porter falters. Wexel was right, his parents were gone, his surrogates were out of state, and his new guardians were offering the opportunity to gain powers that might give him the answers he wanted.

'Fine,' he responds, then taps and swipes, checking each box, ending with a hard squiggle in the signature box that almost dislodges the device from Wexel's hand.

Wexel closes the cover. 'You may proceed.'

Porter picks up the cylinder, angles the pointed end under one nostril, then presses down on the top, emitting a spray that makes his eyes snap open. >>

CHAPTER FIVE
Contact

Porter flinched, returning to the present, unsure how long he'd been 'out'. He was still sitting in the study surrounded by heavy bookcases. Mallory held court in her wingback chair, watching him closely.

He shook a lock of hair from his temple. 'I had another flashback. I think I've got a loose connection... I don't like this toy any more.' He held his head in his hands.

'Relax your mind.'

'I can't. Switch it off,' he demanded.

'Not possible. The particles are still active: you're very receptive. But they'll only stay that way for a small window of time. A matter of hours at most. Long enough to carry out an even more critical task. This time you'll be equipped with a whole suite of abilities,' she offered up. 'If you choose to accept it.'

Porter's eyes drifted.

'Focus, Porter. I need to know if you're in or out.'

He got to his feet, catching a glimpse of himself in a wall mirror: his reflection tired, wan, his eyes bleary.

'I need a second,' he stammered.

Mallory nodded, like a coach that knows their player's hit a ceiling.

Porter left the wood-panelled study and climbed the stairs, his head pounding, then closed the bedroom door behind him, drew the curtains and flopped onto the bed. The ceiling spun. He closed his eyes, trying to regain control of his mind, the room being replaced by the red-tinged blackness behind his lids.

<< Porter angles the cylinder under his other nostril and presses down, emitting a spray that makes him sneeze violently.

'That's the nanoparticles lining your nasal passages,' Ade points out.

Mallory nods. 'Another minute or so and they will have passed through the olfactory nerve. Then we'll have contact.'

Ade retreats, balancing her laptop on her forearm, typing commands. Porter looks around the room with the white walls, not knowing what to expect.

'What does "contact" feel like?' he asks.

'You'll know,' says Mallory.

'Ouch ...' Porter feels a stab of pain in the right side of his head, followed by a tearing sensation that prickles under the skin across his skull, causing him to keel over. His knees buckle, his head lolls between his legs, he sways on his feet, but gravity only makes it worse. 'This is ...'

'Normal,' says Mallory.

Porter manages to peer up, raising his head, then receives another jolt of pain through the temples. He grabs his head in both hands, but wills himself to persevere; the temptation of the powers is too strong to resist.

Mallory doesn't attempt to comfort him; she just watches from a safe distance. 'Listen to me very carefully. I want you to look at the white wall.'

'Which one?'

'Any of them.'

Porter stands, squaring his shoulders, trying to pry open his eyelids, but the room is blinding, like facing into a snowstorm, or the chlorinated water of a swimming pool.

Mallory continues: 'Now I want you to blink.'

'Blink?'

'Just put your lids together ... and blink.'

Porter does as he's been instructed, first hesitantly, like a newborn's first glimpse of the world, then more confidently. 'Okay. Now what?'

Mallory looks to Ade, then they observe Porter, examining the white wall in front of him, as if this is the moment of truth.

'Keep staring at the wall,' Mallory coaxes him.

Ade glances between her laptop screen and Porter, visibly losing faith.

'I'm staring,' says Porter, then feels a wetness in his left nostril, followed by a drip of blood rolling down and gathering on his upper lip. 'What's happening?'

'Stay focused,' orders Mallory.

Porter uses his tongue to wipe away the red rivulet and winces at the sobering metallic taste. He feels his head start to spin, like a fairground ride. He can hear Ade tapping on her laptop in the background. He closes his eyes to block out the noise, feeling a dam of unbidden tears about to break through. 'All right, enough!' He raises his head in despair, searching for the ceiling, wherever that was, then glances down to find something very different in front of him ...

The white wall has transformed into a mountain range of neatly contoured treetops and snowy peaks. The sky is deep blue, above a thin layer of mist - not dissimilar to the landscape he roamed with Joe as a child. He suffers a pang of guilt at the thought of his surrogate parent, and all he's left behind. Porter angles his head in disbelief and the image moves with him in three dimensions, confirmed by a small bird darting from one side of his vision to the other, nestling on a tree branch in the foreground, then taking wing and disappearing. He rubs his eyes, to check he isn't hallucinating. 'What is this ... ?'

Mallory smiles, pleased. 'Adriane chose it. We thought it would remind you of home.'

'It's a screensaver,' says Ade, keeping her eyes on her laptop.

Porter gazes at the wall in awe, seeing the small bird return, darting from the same side of his vision to the other, nestling on the same tree branch, then flying out of frame.

'It's on some kind of loop,' says Porter. 'Did you see that bird?'

Mallory turns to Ade. 'Did we?'

Ade nods, adjusting her natty spectacles, still balancing the laptop on her forearm. 'We did. Though it's smaller on our screen obviously.'

'There it is again,' says Porter, birdwatching. 'Wait. What do you mean, it's smaller on your screen?'

Mallory explains: 'Only *you* are seeing an image projected on that wall, Porter.' She pauses. 'All we see is a white wall.'

Ade continues, 'The image on my laptop is casting to you, through the interface and the olfactory nerve to the domain. Into ... your *brain*. Allow me to demonstrate.' She taps on her trackpad. 'Let's leave the homescreen and go to applications.'

Porter feels his pupils dilate, then his eyes whip up and down, as if following a bouncing ball. In the top-right corner of his vision is a scrolling list of folders and filenames, each with times and datestamps, like the contents of a hard drive.

'Slow down!' he calls out, closing his eyes against the storm of information.

'My bad,' says Ade, lifting her finger off the trackpad.

Porter examines the filenames, picking out words like 'Executive Function', 'Legal' and 'Self-Defence'.

'What are they ... ?' he whispers.

'Applications,' explains Ade. 'Developed by us. All available from the cloud, wherever signal strength allows: the signal conducted by your body's electromagnetic field, that is.'

'You mean I'm online right now?' he asks.

'You've been online, wirelessly, for' - Mallory checks her heavy, stainless-steel watch - 'ninety-six seconds. That's a world record!'

Porter's eyes browse and flicker, hungry for information. 'Okay. What happens next?'

Mallory shrugs, exchanging an excited glance with her colleague. 'What would you like to do next?'

Porter thinks about it, his eyes roaming. 'These applications, you mean I can open them? Use them? In reality?'

Ade walks forward, taking over the presentation. 'As we mentioned before, the cloud sends the data to the domain: your brain. From there, we believe that your natural, limbic adaptability—'

'In a language I can understand, please,' Porter interjects.

Ade carries on: 'That in a young subject like yourself the brain's learning curve is able to adapt quickly to new knowledge and skills ... particularly when placed in a high-stress or survival situation.'

Porter tries to make sense of it. 'Like fight or flight.'

'Something like that.'

Mallory looks to Ade. 'So ... should we take it for a spin?'

Ade moves her finger over the trackpad, highlighting the app list, which appears bright yellow in the top corner of Porter's view.

'The screens are a tool to get you acquainted with the operating system,' she explains. 'Once you get accustomed to it, you'll be able to use available natural terrain to view the files.'

'You mean, blank spaces, buildings, sky, that type of thing ...' says Porter.

'Exactly. Why don't you select an app.'

Porter considers his choices. 'How about martial arts?'

'Predictable,' says Mallory, shaking her head. 'Let's not get ahead of ourselves. I was thinking something more gentle. Like music, or expressive dance.'

'Seriously?' Porter protests.

'It's a good way to measure the brain's coordination with the rest of the body,' Ade agrees. 'Balance, gross motor skills, things of that nature.'

'Fine,' says Porter, disappointed.

'Adriane, maybe you could suggest something?' Mallory asks.

Ade scrolls alphabetically through a list of artists, starting at 'A'. 'Do you like Rick Astley?' she asks.

'I prefer Elvis,' replies Porter.

Mallory nods. 'The King. Good choice.'

'"Suspicious Minds". The original, unmastered version,' he adds.

Ade taps on her trackpad. Porter watches an audio file open up with a timecode running along the lower edge of his view.

Elvis's voice begins crooning in his head.

Porter nods in time, while Mallory and her colleague stand mute, unmoved. He realises they aren't hearing it. It's only in his head.

Ade taps again, activating a new plug-in.

Porter spontaneously feels his hips sway and his legs buckle. 'What?'

Mallory and Ade erupt into laughter as Porter's entire body shakes and gyrates, then drops to one knee, his arm swinging like a lasso. Ade does a joyful leap.

'All right, enough, switch if off!' he demands.

Ade taps again and Porter feels his limbs loosen, releasing the pose.

'Well, that was something!' Mallory tries to hide an elated smile. 'You'll learn to control the apps by yourself. By thought, and by eye movement. Simply blink to confirm.'

Porter ignores her, moves his eyes to select 'A' from the audio files, then blinks. A punchy electronic drum fill launches into 'Never Gonna Give You Up' by Rick Astley. Porter smiles, tucks his hands in his pockets and twirls. Then the music abruptly stops.

Mallory has closed the lid of the laptop. She balances a phone in her other hand, watching it blow up with a series of text messages. 'You passed the first test. Let's see how you do with a real-world one.' She nods to Ade, who reopens the laptop and enters a command, bringing up a threat dashboard. Ade taps on her keyboard, forwarding something over-the-air.

A new window opens before Porter's eyes. An entry flashes up:

Investigate Transcoast Air/Flight 39

It is quickly followed by another line:

Seat 24D, Economy

A message blinks:

Confirmed >>

CHAPTER SIX
Error Message

Porter woke with a stomach-turning feeling of vertigo, recalling the plunging airliner, then sat bolt upright, hearing the bedroom door handle turn.

He willed his eyes to adjust to the dark, but his point of view snowstormed, like a disconnected monitor, then went black, leaving just the vague forms of the bedside table, the dresser, the doorway – a string of icons still glitching, overlaid on his vision.

'Who's there?' he said into the darkness.

'It's me,' a girl's voice answered.

'Maud?' Porter tried to squeeze his eyes into focus, seeing her face emerge under a shard of light at the foot of the bed, the rest of her cast in shadow. 'My eyes . . . don't seem to be working,' he explained.

'Too much screen time, huh.'

'I don't know what you mean.'

'You know exactly what I mean.' She neared the bedside, peering over at him, as if he was under a microscope. 'She's done a real number on you.'

'This isn't helping my headache.'

'Nor is what I'm about to tell you.'

Porter groaned and pulled a pillow over his head, wrapping it around his ears to deaden the sound. The ringing in his ears was similar to the sensation of reaching altitude in the airliner, so much so that he had to remind himself he was still on the ground.

Maud carried on regardless. 'You might think you're pretty special, but you're not the first subject they've tried this on,' she whispered loudly enough for him to hear. 'You probably won't be the last.' She sat at the edge of the bed solemnly, like it was a deathbed.

'Who else . . . ?' he said, his voice muffled.

'Your parents had a colleague.'

Porter emerged from the pillow, hanging on her every word.

'This colleague was suspected of selling the technology into the wrong hands,' she went on. 'That's why they parted ways – he and your parents.'

'How d'you know all this?'

'I see things; I hear things.' She glanced in the direction of downstairs. 'I guess the apple doesn't fall far from the tree. I'm a quick study too. Like you. Except I don't have artificial help . . .'

Porter played dumb, but Maud wasn't fooled.

'I know about *Domain*,' she stated. 'It's a government program. The Department of Machine and Artificial

Intelligence. And they're more concerned with their program than with your head, trust me. You're just their latest' – she took a moment to find the right word – *address*.'

Porter shook his head, trying to make sense of what she was saying. 'It's a trial. It'll wear off in a few hours. I can walk away any time.'

'Is that what they told you?'

'Yeah . . .'

'That's *enough*, Maud.' Her mother's words cut through the dark, messaging her presence, previously unnoticed in the corner of the room.

Maud looked at her mother in defiance. 'You're lying to him. Just like the others—'

'That's *enough*,' Mallory snapped. 'Go to your room. Porter and I need to speak alone.'

Maud scowled, clearly aware of the consequences for non-compliance, then left the bedside and barged past her mother for the door.

Mallory circled the room, turning her attention to her protégé, with the warmth she'd withheld from her daughter. 'How are you feeling? Recharged, I hope?'

Porter lifted his head. 'Ready to pull the plug.'

'Why's that?'

'Because I get the feeling you're lying to me.'

Mallory tutted. 'I told you not to listen to my daughter. She picks up pieces of half-heard conversations, conjures conspiracy theories, weaves them into her own twisted fantasy. If you knew her better, you'd know that the sum of the parts don't always add up.'

'Right now, nothing adds up.'

Mallory soothed him. 'You need to learn to compartmentalise. That means divide your mind into clearly marked spaces, like tools in a toolbox. Or files on a desktop,' she explained. 'It's a quality that normally comes with age. You're still young, the benefit of which is the free flow of data between the brain and the body. You have the ability to learn, to adapt, to grow,' she waxed lyrical. 'Like a Bourbon rose: it's a rather beautiful flower that grows in my hometown.'

She paused before continuing more seriously. 'But you'll also need to be *wise* – which is a quality that transcends age. You have a lot going on in your head. Stay in control of the content. Domain won't dominate your mind . . . unless you allow it to.'

'If you want me to attempt a new task, the answer's no.'

'That's a shame.' She parted the curtains, letting a blinding beam of light into the room. Porter shielded his eyes as she went on, 'Whoever was prepared to down a plane for the sake of one passenger clearly has no regard for innocent life. And will, without doubt, act again. It's not a matter of if but when.'

Mallory waited for guilt to override his reluctance, but Porter stood his ground, suspecting that his boss had already factored in this possibility and would have a response prepared.

Mallory retreated to the doorway. 'I forgot to mention, we have guests. They're downstairs.'

Joe and Sally looked out of place in the formal dining room of Mallory's townhouse, like tourists in a museum, or travellers who'd got off at the wrong stop. Porter felt nausea turn to anger at Mallory for inviting them here, playing them like chess pieces: Joe and Sally being pawns, while she played queen. He grabbed them both in a hug, then took a seat on the opposite side of the dining table.

'I imagine you have some catching up to do,' Mallory announced. 'I'll make coffee.' Her heels clicked across the hall to the kitchen.

'Mallory called last night; she suggested we pay you a visit. We brought some of your things,' said Sally gently. 'That is, unless you want to come home?' There was hope in her voice that maybe his investigation into the past had run its course.

Porter heard a creak from the staircase to the floor above, indicating that Maud was eavesdropping.

Joe remained silent, his eyes roaming the décor, the antique furniture, the oil paintings, anything to distract him from the situation.

'I'm sorry about the way I left,' Porter began.

'We read your note,' Sally whispered. 'A bunch of times.'

Porter turned to Joe to explain. 'I just . . . had to know.' He paused, so badly not wanting to disappoint them. 'I don't have all the answers yet.'

'We understand. Just as long as you don't forget about us,' Sally teased.

Porter shook his head, facing Joe. 'Never.'

'Remember,' Joe chirped up, 'we've still got that buck to catch.'

'If you can shoot straight,' said Porter with a smile.

'I was good once, you were just too young to appreciate it—'

Porter's vision was disrupted by a scrolling ticker of breaking news events, all in red. A mix of images and headlines: an assassination attempt; a hostage situation; a war zone.

Joe seemed overwhelmed with information too: from the madding roar of the car horns outside the window to the richness of the furnishings and the sense of foreboding surrounding the Manhattan townhouse he found himself in. Then there was the burden visibly weighing on Porter's shoulders, bringing with it both wisdom and an agitated distraction beyond his years that made the boy from the mountains almost unrecognisable.

Porter stared through the interference at his surrogate parent. Even though the pair shared no biological connection, and would always be strangers who'd met by chance, Porter felt sick to his stomach at the way he'd left him. 'I want you to know,' he said, 'I think about Tannersville, all the time. The trouble is, every time I do, it feels like it's slipping further away.'

'That's natural,' said Joe.

Porter tried to swipe the ticker away with his eyes. 'No. Like it's vanishing altogether. Like I'm seeing it for the last time.'

Sally looked to Joe, who seemed to sense the desperation in Porter's voice.

'I guarantee,' Joe said, 'whatever happens, we're not going anywhere. Okay . . . ?'

Porter gazed down at Joe and Sally's silhouettes in the backseat of a yellow cab before it pulled away under a row of plane trees, into the afternoon light.

Mallory appeared behind him at the bedroom window. 'They're good people.'

'I know that.'

'Innocent people,' she reminded him. 'Like the ones on that plane.'

Porter knew that calling on his conscience was all part of the plan. He ignored her hollow appeal and recalled Joe's words from the trail: *The best revenge is to live your life, do something good with it.*

'I'm listening,' said Porter, inviting Mallory to continue.

Satisfied that her strategy had worked, she took the ever-present laptop from under her arm and opened it up: 'The person of interest on board Flight 39 was a software engineer by the name of Orin Van Hess. He's a nineteen-year-old upstart – half-German half-Japanese – learned to code before he could walk, graduated from Stanford University and made his fortune by creating a private messaging app.' She tapped the trackpad. 'I'm sending you his file now.'

Porter watched a folder materialise in the corner of his vision. He blinked on it, opening a dropdown of documents and photos, showing a waifish man with black, side-parted hair that Porter vaguely recognised from the rows of sleeping passengers near the front of the plane. Porter didn't need to summon any special abilities to analyse this individual: the likes of Orin Van Hess were splashed across the media weekly, billed as the next kings of the universe. He swiped the folder aside with his eyes, as if it was homework that could be attended to later.

'Where is he now?' Porter asked.

'In protective custody at an undisclosed location.'

'Who wants him dead?' Porter asked. 'Who would ditch an entire airliner for this guy?'

Mallory shrugged. 'That's what we need to find out. Someone gained remote access to the plane. Used the climate control to flood the masks with oxygen, to incapacitate the passengers and crew. Hacked the flight management system with the intention of crashing it. Fortunately, you were able to override it.'

'You put a lot of faith in my abilities.'

'It was a gamble. We needed somebody at short notice, who could blend in. You fit the bill.'

'Thanks,' he said dryly.

'Don't mention it. You took to it like a duck to water – that's why we'd like you to do it again.'

CHAPTER SEVEN
The Party Line

Mallory drew the curtains to ward off prying eyes, then stood by the bureau desk in the corner of the room.

'As I mentioned,' she went on, 'Orin Van Hess developed a private messaging app. It's the gold standard in end-to-end encryption and a favourite for those who prize confidentiality – for better or for worse.'

Porter digested this. A genius whose attention to detail didn't extend to questions of morality or the greater good. None of this was surprising.

Mallory carried on, 'Van Hess recently sold the app to a tech giant called Nordex. You might have heard of it.'

Porter didn't need the string of files in the corner of his eye to tell him: Nordex was fast becoming a household name in the news media and online.

'Sure. They build satellites,' he answered.

'Technically, they're called "satellite constellations",' Mallory explained. 'A dozen or so miniature satellites, launched into low Earth orbit, that work in a similar way to Wi-Fi extenders. They form a chain to provide internet connectivity to hard-to-reach places: remote, indigenous communities ... combat zones.'

Porter didn't like the direction the conversation was taking. 'So where do I come in?'

'The problem is, Nordex recently reached out to the US government to report a leak. It seems Van Hess's super-secure messaging app was breached and someone is using it as a backdoor to sell Nordex data to a foreign power.'

'Embarrassing, but it happens all over the world on a daily basis.'

'Not like this. Due to the nature of what Nordex satellites transmit – from financial data to battlefield orders – it could pose a threat to global security.'

'So what do you want me to do?' he asked.

'Nordex is throwing a party this evening at the New York Public Library. We'd like you to attend.'

'As Porter.com.'

She nodded. 'We believe you'll maintain connection until around midnight. We want you to observe and report. A simple recon mission.'

'Report on what?'

'Adriane will give you the details on the way. Don't worry, if anything goes wrong, you'll be more than equipped to handle it.' She moved for the door. 'Your cover for the event is that your parents work in tech.'

'Easy to remember.'

'We prefer it that way. You better get ready. Your ride will be here in thirty minutes.'

'Wait up . . .' Porter raised a hand. 'If it's a party, what am I supposed to wear?' He glanced at his checked jacket thrown on a nearby chair and his scuffed Nikes below.

She pointed to the closet, then closed the door to his quarters behind her.

Porter fixed his hair and opened the closet door. Inside hung a dark, formal suit, black tie and white collared shirt, brand new and wrapped in plastic. Beneath them was a pair of formal Oxford shoes.

Porter didn't waste time wondering whether they were his size. Everything would be tailored to him, the same as the tech in his head. Thanks to his parents' ingenuity – or *no* thanks to it – he was the property of Domain now.

In a way, perhaps he always had been.

Within twenty minutes, Porter had showered, deodorised and put on the suit. He inspected himself in the mirror: dressed for a party, or a funeral, it was hard to tell which. Hearing a car pull up on the street below, he peered down, expecting to find his ride. Instead, he watched Mallory descend the steps to the kerb, escorting an unwilling Maud, dressed in a puffer jacket and baseball cap. Maud shook off her mother's hand and stood alone at a distance, one boot kicked against the wall.

Wexel struggled down the steps after them, lugging a wheelie bag, which he handed to the driver to stow in the trunk. Maud and her mother exchanged harsh words just out of earshot.

Porter scanned to the top right of his vision and browsed to 'L', searching for 'Lip-Reading'. But before he could blink on it, Maud had already slid into the backseat. Wexel slammed the door behind her, and the town car pulled away into traffic, joining a throng of near-identical vehicles.

Frustrated, Porter left the bedroom, descended the stairs two at a time and found Mallory waiting for him in the entrance hall. 'You brush up well,' she complimented him.

'Where have you sent her?'

'Back to school,' replied Mallory. 'She's too distracted in the city.' Porter looked over his boss's shoulder through the doorway to the street. 'Don't tell me you're hung up on that degenerate daughter of mine?'

Porter shook his head. 'We weren't done talking.' Agitated, he loosened his tie.

'You are now,' she said in her Southern drawl, looking him over. 'So, are you ready to go to the ball?' She ushered him to the front stoop where a black SUV sat at the kerb with a driver standing by the rear passenger door. The backseat was empty, except for a small bottle of water in the armrest.

'Where's my plus one?' he enquired.

'Ade will be with you every step of the way.'

Porter sat alone in the cabin, examining the driver's eyes in the rear-view mirror, then glancing out at the rain-slicked streets, the stream of data in his vision highlighted by passing signs and billboards.

His vision was interrupted by a virtual window that opened up before his eyes, with a thumbnail image of Ade, accompanied by the words: *Adriane – She/Her*. Porter directed his focus to the box and blinked.

A chat window opened with Ade's face inside it, her lips moving but no sound coming from them. She lowered her eyes to her laptop keyboard, tapped, then returned to the webcam. 'Sorry, I was on mute. Can you hear me now?'

'Loud and clear. Like a little voice in my head. Not creepy at all.'

'Super. So you're currently en route to the New York Public Library – that's where the party is being held. With current traffic, your ETA is four minutes.'

'Who's hosting this get-together?'

'Warren Matheson, CEO of Nordex.' She tapped a key, displaying a pop-up of a fifty-something man, dressed in a bomber jacket and jeans, with shiny skin and a shock of spiked hair. 'He's a middle-aged tech bro who did some work for the government in their advanced research and development programs, then went private and formed Nordex. He donates to a number of causes, including both political parties. In fact, he's tipped as a future vice-presidential nominee, maybe even the top position one day. Married twice, one child from each marriage: Olivia and Warren Junior.'

'So what d'you want me to do?' Porter asked.

'According to our intel, a package of leaked information will be handed over at the party. We want you to observe the handover and identify the recipient of that information: "the bagman".'

'What type of package? A bag? A briefcase?'

'We don't know the nature of the package . . . or its contents. We only know that the handover will take place this evening at exactly 20:11 hours in the Rose Main Reading Room.'

'Then what?'

'Follow the package.'

'Where?'

'Wherever it leads.'

'Until midnight, when I turn into a pumpkin presumably.'

'Hopefully not a pumpkin,' she replied, then checked her screen. 'It looks like you've arrived.'

The SUV joined a row of vehicles idling on Fifth Avenue at the base of the broad steps to the New York Public Library. Porter opened the rear passenger door and stepped out into light rain, making his way up the stairway between a pair of stone lions, then under the majestic columns to the security line, which was filled with guests in a mix of tailored suits and designer outfits. Porter had always felt he was on the outside of every party, looking in – and this was no different. On the outside, looking in, with somebody talking to him in his head. Not weird at all.

'Give your name to the doorman. You're on the list,' Ade coaxed him from the pop-up window.

'The name's Porter Simms,' he said to the bulky man in a black shirt guarding the entrance. 'My parents are inside?' The man looked him over, examined the guest list for a moment, then opened the velvet rope without remark.

Porter walked into a secure area, trying not to be distracted by the voice in his head. A security guard guided him through a metal detector, then waved a wand over his body to check for devices.

'No phone?' the guard asked.

'I'm on a digital detox.'

'Not yet you're not,' said Ade from the corner of his vision.

The security guard shrugged, unaware of the battery of weapons in Porter's head, then ushered him into a grand marble foyer, lit by lanterns and candelabras.

'By the way,' she added, 'seeing as you're basically a walking Wi-Fi device, don't be surprised if your signal interferes with other devices. You're like any smartphone.'

'Better than being a dumb phone, I guess.'

'Infinitely better. Take the right-hand staircase,' said Ade in his head. Porter did as he was told, climbing the carved stone staircase that seemed to float upwards unsupported. 'Go to the third floor,' she added.

'Okay,' he answered to nobody in particular, then caught sight of the time in a corner of his 'virtual desktop'. It read: 19:59. Twelve minutes to game time.

He followed the procession of guests up the staircase, past the second floor, where marble passageways extended off in both directions, then proceeded to the third, where the space opened up into a rotunda, framed by soaring arches, muralled walls and wood panelling.

'I'm here,' he replied.

Ade's face hovered at her laptop screen. 'Proceed right, to the Catalogue Room.'

'Will do.'

'Excuse me?' a girl's voice interjected, having overheard him.

Porter turned to find a striking-looking teenage girl standing beside him. She was maybe fifteen, with spiked, platinum-blonde hair in a crew-cut, dressed in a designer skirt with an oversized tux jacket and white dress shirt. Her gaze and bearing made her seem older than her years; someone for whom the party was boring and routine. The overall effect was that Porter felt completely outclassed.

'Sorry,' Porter pretended, 'I have a habit of talking to myself.'

'Ditto,' the girl responded, examining him, then extended her hand. 'I'm Olivia. Matheson.'

Porter nodded, already knowing this, having glimpsed Ade tapping at her keyboard in the corner of his eye, posting an archived image of the girl from a previous launch event. It was a positive match.

Olivia broke the awkward pause. 'And you are . . . ?'

He shook her hand, which was pale as alabaster, with sunflower-yellow fingernails. 'Porter.'

The pop-up in the corner of his eye glitched and fizzled, causing Ade's image to cut out.

'You're getting distracted,' Ade snapped in his head. 'Stay focused or you're going to lose contact.'

'Is something wrong?' Olivia asked sympathetically. 'Are you feeling all right?'

'Never felt better.' Porter blinked, closing the pop-up window with Ade in it.

'Who are you here with?' Olivia enquired.

'My parents. They're in tech,' he delivered the rehearsed line.

Olivia nodded, accepting his explanation. 'Me too. In fact, my dad's hosting this shindig.' She turned in the direction of a teen boy in a tux with slicked-back hair, unwisely picking at the low-hanging fruit of a pyramid-shaped food stand. 'That doofus over there is my brother. Well, half-brother technically.'

Porter nodded, already knowing this too. 'It's hard to define family sometimes.'

'Agree one hundred percent.' She glanced around the room, looking for her own.

'Quite a party,' Porter observed.

She shrugged. 'I'm not a fan of the penguin suit' – she straightened the lapel of her tux jacket – 'but the desserts are killer. I'm heading over there now if you want to join me?'

Porter glanced at his internal clock, which was now showing 20:06. Five minutes to go. Out of time.

'Actually, I was just trying to find my parents,' he lied.

'Once again, me too.' She scanned the crowd of stylish but anonymous faces. 'My dad's about to speak. I need to go find a corner to hide in.'

'I know the feeling.'

'Maybe I'll see you later?'

Porter nodded. 'For sure.'

'Super.' She smiled and turned to face the sea of guests.

'Okay . . .' said Porter, more or less to himself, as Olivia melted into the crowd. He looked after her a moment, then came to his senses and blinked to reopen the chat window. 'I'm here.'

'Oh, welcome back,' said Ade with irritation.

'You wouldn't want to blow my cover, would you?'

'We're running out of time, *Romeo*. The Catalogue Room,' she reminded him, providing a floor plan of the building in the corner of his vision. 'It leads to the Rose Main Reading Room. That's the drop point.'

'On my way.'

CHAPTER EIGHT
Contactless Delivery

Porter crossed the Catalogue Room, past rows of long oak tables with brass reading lamps and computer terminals, the air heavy with the smell of leather book jackets and floor polish. The chairs were all empty, the readers gone for the day, the books lining the walls now just for decoration. Porter recognised the layout from the floor plan, passing through a small foyer that opened into the Rose Main Reading Room: a cavernous space, larger than a basketball court, with over twenty rows of tables and chairs, and a generous walkway running down the middle of them. Books lined each wall, around which the hundred or so guests mingled. Above them, matching chandeliers were suspended from a fifty-two-foot-high gilded ceiling with murals of heavenly clouds parting to reveal a golden sun. Porter scanned the room, detecting nothing that looked obviously like a package being prepared for delivery.

'Go to the gallery – you'll get a better view,' Ade said in his head.

Porter saw a raised balcony running along the perimeter of the room. The narrow gallery was deserted except for a further line of bookcases. He passed the book return office and climbed a short staircase to the gallery level.

Without warning, the chandeliers across the room dimmed to near darkness, leaving only the warm, orange arcs of the reading lamps. Soft classical music started playing from a string quartet in one corner. A spotlight shone down on the walkway between the desks, picking out a middle-aged man in a silvery suit with an open shirt, no tie, standing centre stage in the chamber. Porter recognised him as the CEO of Nordex, Warren Matheson.

'Good evening!' Matheson's voice rang out, and the murmur of guests tapered off. 'Thanks for coming to my party!'

The audience cheered and raised their glasses.

Porter realised why Olivia might have seemed embarrassed by her father. The man was handsome enough, with his shock of spiked hair and chiselled jaw, but he wore the conceited pout of an overgrown child.

Matheson continued his rehearsed speech: 'You all know me as a numbers guy. Zeros and ones mostly. But I do appreciate words, even if I don't normally manage more than two hundred and eighty characters at a time.' Peals of laughter. 'That's why I invited you here . . . to a library.'

He spread out his arms, embracing the space. 'Libraries spread knowledge to people. Just like our Nordex satellite constellations. Bringing data to those in need . . . whether they're downloading an episode of *Friends* in the Arctic Circle, or receiving a mission brief in a far-off battlefield. We are committed to *connection*.'

A ripple of applause travelled through the crowd.

'As a symbol of that commitment,' he went on, 'in twenty-four hours we'll be opening a Nordex Campus in one of the Big Apple's most deserving, and least privileged, boroughs.'

He pointed off to the side of the room and the spotlight trailed in the same direction to rest on a scale model of a modern-looking building: a dramatic, glass dome, with one side of it hollowed out to create a mezzanine overlooking a lush Amazonian garden. Tall trees nestled among dense, jungle vegetation and water features, centring on the smooth, still surface of a reflection pool.

'It will be a hub of learning, training and jobs,' he announced. 'I intend to prove to this city that tech has the power to bring people together, even when so many seek to divide us.'

In the gallery, Porter stopped paying attention to the words floating up and used his vantage point to scan the crowd.

'Anything?' asked Ade, checking in.

'Nothing.'

Guests lounged among the stacks of books. None stood out. There was no sign of a package; no tic or tell that might indicate a messenger. He rechecked his internal clock, which showed 20.10. One minute to go. The applause lulled.

'Thank you,' Matheson concluded. 'Now, I think I'm way over my character limit. So please . . . sit back and enjoy the show.'

The host jogged out of the spotlight in a show of good health.

Porter watched him go, then squinted as an explosion of colour filled the chamber below, accompanied by strobing lights and the thudding bass of a sound system. Spotlights illuminated the full length of the walkway while a dozen fashion models emerged from the entrance in garish, sci-fi-inspired outfits with shoulder pads, cut-out sections and oversized boots. Spectators excitedly raised their phones in unison to record the event.

Porter sank back into the shadows, overwhelmed by visual information, peering over the handrail, as his clock clicked to 20:11. 'Standing by.'

He winced as a storm of flash bulbs went off, but detected nothing unusual, just guests exchanging sidelong comments as the fashion show proceeded.

The models marched to the end of the room, performed practised turns and returned the way they'd come. Then Porter faltered, his attention caught by a female model in a black dress, who spun to reveal a bold, black-and-white design splashed across her back. Porter blinked, inadvertently highlighting the design on his 'virtual desktop' for a split second.

'Damn it,' he cursed, then got a jolt, experiencing a rush of information that made his neck snap back. His brain appeared to be receiving the file. He felt the rush slow down as the data stream completed. 'It's a QR code,' he hollered to Ade.

'What?' she responded.

'The package.'

Then Porter's head turned, noticing a sudden, random movement in the crowd. Among the onlookers was a *figure dressed in black* under a baseball cap and mask – noticeable only because the stranger's head had also snapped back, just like Porter's, as if receiving the same data stream.

'I-I . . .' Porter stammered. 'I think I just witnessed the drop.'

'I don't understand. What are you seeing?'

'I don't know either. But I think the package was delivered over-the-air,' he answered.

The figure in black snapped back to a normal standing position, neck straight, composed, then wheeled around and started off in the direction of the exit.

'I'm going after the bagman,' said Porter.

'You're only there to observe. Await further instruction,' Ade replied.

Porter ignored her, running back along the gallery, jumping down the short set of stairs to the library floor and landing in a heap with the spotlight straying over his back.

From across the chamber, the figure spotted Porter's sprawled form lit up for a moment. Putting two and two together, the figure sprinted for the exit staircase, pushing past audience members, scattering them like bowling pins. Porter ducked out of the spotlight, making his way around the edge of the crowd, running past the stacks.

'What's your status?' Ade barked.

'In pursuit.'

'What?!'

'Stand by. I might need you.'

'Wait, you don't give the orders—'

The figure in black burst through the doorway of the Catalogue Room into a traffic jam of fashionistas. An overenthusiastic male designer grabbed the figure by the shoulders: 'Mister, I just *love* your outfit—' The figure punched out the admirer, prompting gasps, then barged into a catering area with trays of appetisers, crystal and silverware arranged on white tablecloths.

Waiters and guests scattered as the figure leaped onto a banquette, using it as a springboard to hop onto the row of tables, stepping from one to the next, sending cutlery clanking and glasses crashing, to the consternation of onlookers.

Porter stepped over the prone designer to see the figure dive-roll from the last table to the stone floor at the far end, rolling to an upright position to arrive at the main staircase. The figure then sat sideways on the edge of the bannister and sailed downwards to the next floor with perfect balance.

Porter accelerated to a sprint, weaving past the upended tables to reach the rotunda, in time to see the figure hop off the end of the bannister at the floor below.

Ade gestured from the pop-up in the corner of his eye. 'Hold your position. We're locking down the building.'

Ignoring her, Porter tried to balance himself on the bannister, sliding about halfway down, then toppling backwards into mid-air, landing fortuitously on a sofa below. His 'virtual desktop' fizzed and reloaded. He struggled to his feet.

The figure raced around the landing to the next staircase, only to be met by a trio of bouncers jogging up the steps in formation. The figure hesitated, appearing to receive some new instruction, then spun and pushed through a fire exit. The bouncers trailed the suspect through the door. Seconds later, Porter followed suit, entering an access corridor.

He found the three bouncers laid out at angles, flat on the floor: unconscious. The fire door at the end of the corridor slowly swung to; a cool breeze gusted through it. Porter raced for the doorway, finding a small stretch of flat roof with a row of air conditioning extractor fans, leading to a sheer drop with skyscrapers and treetops beyond. Porter edged towards the stone balustrade, gazing down the outer face of the building, expecting to see the figure escaping, but there was nobody there – only a team of security staff on the ground, forming an ant-like perimeter around the wide, stone steps of the entrance.

Then he heard a scratching sound and tracked it, incredulous, to find the suspect free-climbing a sheer wall adjacent to the main entrance, wedging themselves into one of the architraves around the edge of the library windows.

'What the . . . ?' The wind picked up, drowning out Porter's voice.

The suspect turned towards a mighty stone column that extended three storeys down to the ground, then jumped from the architrave into mid-air, obtaining a hold on the knurled channels carved into the circumference of the pillar. Porter watched – feeling nauseous at the sight of it – then located a course of bevelled bricks protruding from the corner of the building, offering him a parallel route downwards. He whipped his eyes to the corner of his vision: to the pop-up with Ade in it.

'I need help.'

'Oh, *now* you want to talk,' she remarked.

'Suspect's currently on the second floor. Or should I say *outside* the second floor.'

CHAPTER NINE
Escape

Porter spiralled into vertigo, watching the figure scuttle down the stone column in a swift descent. Porter's perspective distorted, the ground appearing to fall away beneath him. He looked up to the corner of his eye where Ade was busily typing, then a bank of files scrolled alphabetically, until he slowed them with his mind, stopping to blink on a particular file, which was highlighted: 'Free Solo Climbing'.

Connecting...

Porter experienced a tingle of muscle memory, like pins and needles, then reached for the stone balustrade and swung himself over it, grabbing one of the vertical balusters, feeling his stomach sink as he dangled by one hand like a pendulum. The three-storey drop yawned below him, daring him to look down. Instead, he extended his foot to press against the cornerstone of the wall, steadying himself, while his free hand searched the bevelled surface of the bricks, burying his fingers into the slim groove between them. Balanced on two fingers, he swung across, coming face to face with the course of bricks, pressing the toe of his shoe into a crevice.

'Where are you now?' demanded Ade from the pop-up.

'In the air.'

'In the air where?'

'It's probably better if I don't look down.'

He made his descent, moving his hands then feet alternately to find the next hold.

From below, the suspect peered up in surprise for a moment, then slid down the remainder of the column, landing in a perfectly executed squat on the ground.

Porter paused to glance down, seeing the suspect jogging across the green expanse of Bryant Park towards 41st Street, overhung by plane trees.

Porter shook his head, breathless. 'Bagman's still on the move.'

Porter reached a first-floor window and dropped the last few metres to the ground, landing hard. He wiped his hands on his trousers, brushed stone dust from his suit jacket and started across the wet grass, which was lit up like a sports field by the chequerboard of lights from surrounding skyscrapers.

Reaching the far end, the bagman extended a keyfob, aiming it at a row of parked cars. A black Porsche 911 Turbo blinked in response and the figure dived into the driver's seat.

Porter barrelled down the steps from Bryant Park, hurdled a guard rail and reached the kerb, a second too late.

Smoke poured from the Porsche's wheel arches as it peeled out along 41st Street under the canyon of office buildings. Porter looked around helpless, then spotted a uniformed valet parker standing nearby, in conversation with the owner of a red Ferrari Spider sat idling outside a restaurant.

Porter straightened his dark suit and tie, then sauntered up to the open car window.

'Excuse me, sir, but I've always wanted to sit in a Ferrari.'

The owner looked him up and down, then grinned and undid his seat belt. 'Sure, why not?'

Porter waited for the man to climb out, then blinked.

Connecting...

Porter slipped behind the steering wheel, pressed the seat adjustment, smiled at the owner, then thumbed the switch on the wheel to Race mode and flicked the paddle shifter into gear, slamming his foot on the accelerator. The steering wheel spun in his hands until he wrestled control, fishtailing out of the valet area, taking off down 41st after the Porsche.

On the dashboard, the rev counter leaped and the digits raced upwards, the power pressing Porter's head into the headrest. The car's owner was reduced to a frantically waving figure in the droplet-shaped wing mirror as Porter saw the streetlights race by on either side, the road narrowing before his eyes. He checked the signal bars in the corner of his vision, alongside Ade.

'I won't ask,' she remarked.

Porter swerved around another vehicle, blew through a stoplight and pinpointed the suspect's black sportscar two blocks ahead, weaving through traffic. 'He's still on the move.'

'Apparently so. At three times the speed limit,' Ade pointed out.

Porter cut the wheel left and right, swerving around a freewheeling shopping cart, then floored the accelerator again, until a blaze of red and blue lights lit up the rear-view mirror, reflecting into his eyes. The wail of sirens could be heard behind the growl of the Ferrari's engine. Porter squinted, glancing between the cop car closing on him from behind and the Porsche still moving ahead at a high rate of speed.

Porter flicked the paddle shifter down a gear and veered onto a side street, banking left down an alleyway, parallel to 41st. The Ferrari sped past garbage dumpsters and abandoned cardboard boxes. The cop car drifted around the corner behind him in a screech of rubber, unable to close the gap. Porter watched the digits on the dashboard race up, accompanied by a flurry of warning lights as he careered out of the alley in a trail of sparks, rejoining 41st.

Hurled left then right, Porter corrected the steering wheel, gritting his teeth, finding the Porsche in his sights. Porter pressed harder on the accelerator, hearing the Ferrari's gearbox change up twice by itself, closing on the target, until a shape blocked his path.

A garbage truck reversed out of nowhere.

Porter stepped on the brake pedal with both feet, bracing for impact. The Ferrari slid sideways, its tyres making high-pitched yelps in a controlled skid, leaving four black marks etched into the road surface, coming to rest inches from the belly of the truck. The driver sounded an angry horn blast. In the gap below the undercarriage, Porter spied the Porsche flash its taillights defiantly and escape down a side street out of sight.

Porter heard a screech of tyres behind him, followed by the shouts of two cops running to the driver window with sidearms drawn.

'Hands on the wheel! Where I can see 'em,' the lead cop yelled.

Porter switched off the car and obeyed their instructions, then looked up to the right of his vision and *blinked*.

The cop pulled open the door. 'I'm arresting you under New York Traffic Code Section 509, reckless driving while underage without a licence. Step out of the vehicle.'

Porter craned his neck up from the driver's seat. 'I have the right to an attorney.'

'Step out of the vehicle,' the cop repeated.

'Am I under arrest, officer? If so, you'll need to "Mirandize" me first.'

'Okay, wise guy, let me read your Miranda rights: you have the right to remain silent. Anything you say *can* and *will* be used against you in a court of law. Now . . . exit the vehicle with your hands in the air.'

'I'm finding your tone unduly aggressive and triggering. I'd like a parent or legal guardian present. This constitutes harassment of a minor.'

The lead cop looked to his partner with eyebrows raised. 'Are you for real?'

'I guess we'll find out in court,' said Porter.

At that moment, a black SUV pulled up alongside him and the rear door opened to reveal Mallory, dressed in a long, black overcoat, holding out a leather wallet that flipped open to reveal a government ID.

'It's all right, officer, we'll take it from here.' She gestured for Porter to stay put.

The cop inspected the ID, perplexed, then looked to his partner.

Mallory flashed them a smile. 'Thank you for your cooperation.'

'Have a pleasant evening, officers,' Porter said from the driver's seat.

The officers holstered their weapons and returned to their cop car, which blipped its sirens, pulled a U-turn and left the street deserted, lit by the arc of a streetlamp.

Mallory went to lean on the roof of the sportscar, not amused. 'You lost him.'

Ade leaned her head out of the backseat of the SUV, her ever-present laptop resting on her knee. 'On the plus side, you proved very effective at deploying the apps. In fact, you outperformed expectations by over two hundred percent. Even if the end result was suboptimal.'

Porter slumped back in his seat. 'I just had my head pumped full of zeros and ones. You should try it sometime.'

'Allow us to unpack some of those for you,' said Mallory.

He looked at her, puzzled. What should have come off as maternal concern sounded more like tech support: as if he was a device instead of a human being.

Ade explained from her workspace in the backseat of the SUV: 'You inadvertently captured the QR code, on the runway in the library. We need you to send it over-the-air to us,' she instructed. 'You'll find it in your dock. Top left of your vision.'

Porter raised his eyes, searching the task bar in his head. 'The bagman captured it too. Judging by his body language, he might even have some version of what I'm using.'

'That's impossible,' Mallory stated.

'Maybe, but I'm just telling you what I saw.'

'Share the file,' Mallory ordered. 'If we know what's being leaked, then we at least have a ghost of a chance of figuring out what it means.'

Porter's eyes came to rest on the dock, where he located the QR code sitting innocently in the corner. He blinked on it, opening a small file icon, then tried to drag it with his eyes towards the Wi-Fi icon. The file kept sticking and whipping back to its original location. He tried again, craning his eyes and blinking. The file flashed and a spinning wheel indicated:

Sending...

'I think I did it,' he said.

Ade watched her screen, seeing the QR code arrive in all its black-and-white, hieroglyphic glory. 'Gotcha.' She clicked on it.

A single word appeared on her screen: *Encrypted* . . .

Ade sighed, 'This may take some time.'

'We don't have the luxury of time,' said Mallory, concerned.

Porter checked his internal clock. It read: 22:53. 'I've still got an hour left – let's make the most of it.' He started the Ferrari, the engine burbling, but Mallory's expression darkened. 'What haven't you told me?' he asked her.

CHAPTER TEN
Going Offline

Porter switched off the car to hear her better. The engine sputtered out, making a series of ticks as it cooled down. Mallory hesitated, as if deciding how much to reveal.

'US Cyber Command is a wing of the Defense Department that monitors threats in cyberspace. They've been watching Nordex for a while. They recently intercepted online "chatter".' She paused to explain: 'That's slang for messages passed between the leaker and whoever is buying the leaked data.'

Porter knew about chatter. It was the lifeblood of modern intelligence work: the wholesale scouring of social media and online forums for clues or keywords, which were then vacuumed up by the government for analysis, in order to detect threats before they became reality.

Mallory carried on, 'Naturally, this buyer has cloaked themselves in aliases and phony IP addresses. Which means we can't discover their identity or pinpoint their location. But, according to analysts, the chatter suggests the leak could be part of a bigger event of some kind. Not a cyber attack. A potentially catastrophic real-world event.'

Porter realised. 'And I lost the bagman.'

Ade chimed in from her workstation in the backseat of the SUV. 'Yes, but everybody leaves a trail of digital breadcrumbs. We just got a hit on the licence plate of the Porsche. It just entered the Lincoln Tunnel. Bagman used a cloned credit card to pay the toll. If we get lucky, he'll use it again.'

Mallory shook her head, circling the car, gaming out the scenario. 'Bagman's using the tunnel to switch vehicles. Then he'll switch cards. If he's half as resourceful as you described, he'll have already made the handover, will check in at Newark International and be anywhere in the world within a few hours.'

Frustrated, she felt her phone ring, tapped it and placed it to her ear, retreating under a streetlight for privacy. 'Sweetie?' Porter heard her say. 'Okay. Stay where you are. I'm on my way. Okay, bye.' She paced back to the SUV and spoke to the driver.

'Something wrong?' Porter asked.

'Maud was involved in a collision on the way to school. She's shaken up, but she's okay.' Mallory climbed into the backseat next to Ade, and Porter realised he wasn't invited along for the ride. She called back to him: 'Think you can get yourself home in one piece?'

'I'll manage.' Porter pressed 'Start' and revved the engine, aggravated.

'Don't worry, we'll be tracking you.'

Mallory's SUV swung a U-turn and accelerated up the street, receding in his rear-view mirror. Porter flicked the paddle shifter into gear and prepared to pull away, when he was interrupted by a black fingernail tapping on the opposite window. He powered it down to find a familiar face gaping in.

'Mau—?' he said, incredulous.

She extended her arm, holding a finger to his lips, to indicate silence, then reached for the door handle and let herself into the passenger side. She was still wearing the puffer jacket, baseball cap and jackboots she'd had on when she left the townhouse.

She pointed in the direction of downtown. 'Drive.'

Porter put the car into gear and did what she asked.

'Porter, do you read me?' Ade's voice arrived via the chat window in his head.

Maud made a cut-throat gesture from the passenger seat.

Porter improvised, 'Erm, signal's spotty right now. I think I'm losing you . . .'

'You're heading in the wrong direction. Do you read?' Ade pointed out.

Maud jabbed her finger through the windshield at the illuminated stairwell of a subway station a block ahead of them. Then she removed something from the backpack nestled between her knees. 'Put this on,' she instructed in a whisper.

It was a black Yankees baseball cap.

'Why?'

'Just do it.'

Porter adjusted the band and put the cap on, keeping one hand on the wheel.

'Porter?' Ade's voice fizzled. The pop-up with her face in it blipped off, leaving his vision clear of information.

'You're offline,' said Maud, tapping on the window as they approached the run-down station. 'Pull over here.'

Losing contact, Porter stalled the Ferrari, forgetting how to control it, and lurched to a halt outside the entrance. Bystanders shook their heads at him from the sidewalk.

Maud looked down, embarrassed, and got out. 'By the way, where did you get this ridiculous car?'

'I thought—'

'I'd like it?'

'No, I thought you were—'

'I gave them the slip. Distracted the driver, caused a bit of a scrape. He's banged up, but he'll be fine.'

'But why?'

'So we could talk, silly. I'll tell you on the way.' She beckoned him to follow her down the lit stairwell below ground to the subway.

'On the way where?' he asked but followed her anyway.

She seemed to exert a gravitational pull on him that was stronger than anything else in his head. She took deliberate strides, her jackboots making faint squeaks on the tiled floor as he followed her deeper into the station. She hopped over the turnstiles, signalling Porter to do the same, then led him down an escalator to a platform, dotted with CCTV cameras and departure boards.

A train was waiting with its doors open, about to depart. Maud took his hand and led him into the train car. The automatic doors closed behind them and the train pulled away.

Porter sat in the darkened carriage, feeling the tracks rattling under their seats, causing their knees to vibrate and collide, unsure whether he was supposed to look at his captor or not. It made no difference, as he was a willing hostage. The train picked up speed and Porter stared ahead, catching glimpses of their own reflections in the windows.

'How d'you find me?' he asked.

'It wasn't difficult. My mom calls me a technophobe, but I know enough to be dangerous. I paid the class geek to install a tracker on her phone, disguised as a cat meme. I mean, who can resist?' She smirked at her ingenuity. 'Speaking of which, keep your head down, we're still on camera.'

Porter pulled down the brim of his baseball cap, which was at odds with his suit jacket and shirt. 'What is this thing? A tinfoil hat?'

'It's far more effective than tin,' said Maud, 'but lighter than lead. It contains a fine steel mesh, sort of a homemade Faraday cage that disturbs electromagnetic fields and stops the data stream.'

Porter nodded, impressed. 'In any case, it'll switch off when the particles wear off, right?' She didn't respond, the noise of the tracks drowning them out.

The doors routinely opened and closed as passengers boarded and disembarked. The train emerged from underground, becoming quieter, revealing an uneven scatter of neon lights from surrounding boroughs outside the windows. Uncomfortable with the silence, Porter turned his head a fraction in Maud's direction.

'Where exactly are we going?'

'Somewhere off the grid, away from all the noise.'

Porter held his tongue as the train rumbled on, arriving at the Jamaica station in the borough of Queens, where, without a word, he followed Maud out of the carriage across a platform to an escalator. They climbed the moving stairway, hastily exiting the station through a parking lot, before deviating through a series of dark, deserted back streets lined with nondescript, sparsely lit apartment buildings and occasional auto body shops, barred up for the night. The moisture in the air mixed with oil-based emissions from nearby businesses to form a shimmering miasma on the skyline. Although drab, the concrete walls were free of streaming data or pop-up windows, and for that reason appeared strangely fresh and bright. As well as the terrain being cleared of augmented reality, Porter's mind felt clearer, calmer, with more blank space for thought, without the clutter of information.

Maud stopped a moment, her dark skin and green eyes lit by a corner streetlamp. 'What did she tell you about the side effects? My mother?'

'That it can cause flashbacks. That after twenty-four hours the particles will wear off . . .'

'When did she tell you that?' Maud asked.

Porter looked up at an old street clock over a building: it was after midnight. 'Over twenty-four hours ago,' he replied, looked back at her, confused, a dark thought dawning on him, sending a shiver up his spine.

He lifted the brim of his cap a moment and the sky illuminated with several virtual windows loading up. Maud stopped his hand and pulled the brim down. The windows blipped off again.

'Why am I still online?' he questioned her.

She looked to the side, not wanting to meet his eyes, then resolved to tell him. 'Because the particles *don't* wear off, Porter. Once they're introduced into your bloodstream, they're there forever. It's a type of gene therapy. I'm not fully versed in the science, but I know they're there for good. There's no going back.' She studied him for signs of a reaction, finding only a blank stare. 'I'm sorry to be the one to tell you.'

Porter swallowed, then shook it off. 'You say that like it's a bad thing. I mean, I'm still master of my domain, in control of my own mind, I just get the enhanced version. Smarter, faster, more efficient. Twenty-four-seven access to anything I want. I mean, it makes me close to superhuman.'

She looked at him with scarcely disguised pity.

'Right?'

'Porter . . . If you've read any comic books, you'll know that for every superpower there's a downside. Usually quite a major downside.'

'So?' he demanded. 'Don't keep me in suspense. What is it?'

'The human brain wasn't built to deal with the continual bombardment of data. You must've seen the studies. It increases dopamine levels, overloads reward pathways, dulls your emotional response, messes with your mind. And, in your case, it's next-level screen time we're talking about.'

'How about you put it in a language I can understand *without* an app?' he countered. 'No offence, but you're starting to sound like your mom.'

'None taken,' she answered chillingly. 'I'll put it simply. The human brain is faster and more versatile than any man-made processor on Earth, even the ones as big as a sports field . . . but the brain still has its limitations. Like any device.'

'Such as?'

'Memory capacity.'

'I don't know what you mean,' he said with growing apprehension.

'Every time you use one of the skillsets, it takes up space in your frontal lobe, where memories are stored.'

'Like RAM,' Porter murmured, repeating what Maud's mother, Mallory, had told him.

Maud nodded. 'Random Access Memory. The brain relies on it, just like a computer. And when that capacity gets full, it has to *delete* something.'

'You're telling me, every time I use the powers, I'm losing my memory?'

'Not in big chunks, no. But over time – they don't know how long – *yes*. You will erode your own naturally formed memories. And with them, your own sense of self,' she explained softly, her tone relenting again, turning to pity. 'They will be replaced by skills, at the expense of empathy, feelings. At that point, Domain will control *you*, not the other way around. And you may not have your emotions or intuition to fall back on.'

Mallory's words echoed back to him: *Domain won't dominate your mind . . . unless you allow it to.* What she didn't tell him was that over time, this would be inevitable. His memories would fade and Domain would reign supreme.

Porter looked around at the bleak street of barred gates and razor-wire fences, feeling the walls closing in on him. He was suddenly more afraid of being at ground level than he was dangling from a rooftop defying gravity. 'This can't be happening.'

'It's already happened,' Maud responded. 'Now we need to get you offline for a while, try to repair some of the damage. Live in the moment for as long as we can.'

'What about the mission?' In his absence, Mallory would be waiting for Ade's decryption of the QR code, to figure out the nature of the threat they faced.

'Relax, I used some old-fashioned detective work,' replied Maud. 'I'll tell you on the way.'

He was so lost that he'd stopped asking where.

CHAPTER ELEVEN
Return To Home

The destination sign on the front of the bus lit up in orange pixels over a black background, displaying 'East Hampton'.

Porter and Maud climbed aboard and shuffled towards the back of the hulking vehicle with their heads down, among a handful of late-night travellers. They sank into their seats with Porter nearest the window, resting his aching brow against the glass which gave on to pure blackness and the faint reflection of his own worn features under the brim of the baseball cap. The vehicle's long windscreen wipers flicked away rain as the engine rumbled to life and it proceeded through the streets of Queens, travelling eastwards out of the city.

The vibration of the bus through the window lulled Porter to sleep.

<< He sits at his desk by the bedroom window in Tannersville. Treetops extend into the distance under

the evening light. He lets his eyes defocus, the rows of pines promising endless possibilities, all out of reach.

He overhears snippets of a conversation from downstairs, just able to make out familiar words and phrases in the uppermost frequencies of his hearing.

'We can't keep him here forever ...' says Sally. 'It's not fair on him.'

'Don't you think I know ...' Joe responds, downbeat.

'The school keep asking questions ... He doesn't even look like us.'

'If he leaves,' Joe ponders, 'we don't know what might happen. What he might be walking into.'

Porter looks down at his desk, where a space has been cleared, all his half-finished homework, books and magazines moved to one side. Three items remain: Mallory's business card with the insignia ISS, International Social Service, over an address ending in 'NY, NY'; next to that, a Greyhound bus ticket with the destination 'New York City'; finally, a blank piece of paper with the words 'Dear Joe' handwritten at the top.

He picks up his pen, then is interrupted by a knock.

'Porter?'

'Yeah?'

Porter turns the page over, covering the items, as Joe's head peeks through the doorway.

Joe senses something different about the boy: a maturity that wasn't there before, poorly disguised by the attempt at secrecy. He forgives him, already knowing what it means. 'I always taught you to follow your instincts,' Joe points out.

Porter nods, playing it off with a smile. 'Only fools rush in.'

Joe knows what's really going on in his head. 'Whatever you decide, we'll understand.'

'Lighten up.' Porter gets up to stand opposite him, then wrestles him, grabbing him in a hug. 'Think you can get rid of me that easy?' he says into the nap of Joe's shirt, but his eyes are wet, straying out of the window.

'It's okay, son.' Joe feels the word tumble out, unable to help himself. He only used it occasionally - usually by accident.

Porter wants so badly to use the word 'Dad', but it still doesn't feel right, even now.

'Let's talk it over in the morning, okay?' Joe suggests.

'Okay.'

Joe retreats to the door and closes it behind him, leaving Porter alone with his thoughts.

Later that night, Porter watches the lights of passing cars move across the posters on his bedroom wall. He swings his legs out of bed and feels the carpet under his feet.

Across the hall, Joe wakes, hearing a noise from downstairs, then checks his watch: 4:07 a.m. Leaving Sally undisturbed, he creeps out of bed and opens the door, seeing something waiting on the landing carpet: a folded letter. Nauseous, Joe hesitates, then picks it up and reads the contents, his lips moving silently. His head drops as he approaches the window overlooking the driveway.

Porter is already halfway up the road, walking with purpose in the direction of Main Street, wearing his checked jacket, carrying a hold-all bag slung across his back. He turns back, thinking he can see something through the frost in the upstairs window, but he can't tell. Porter feels a chill, blows into his cupped hands to warm them, then traipses into the distance. >>

Porter woke with a start as the bus slowed hard, approaching an off-ramp. Maud sat sentry like a night owl beside him.

'Bad dream?' she asked.

'Random memory,' he answered. 'They're still happening, even now I'm offline.'

Maud nodded. 'That's why we're taking this trip. To ease your mind, try to piece you back together.'

Before he could question her any further, she had moved on.

'So. While you were chasing around Manhattan, I've been doing some homework of my own,' she said. 'On Nordex.'

'How do you know about that? How d'you know any of this?'

'The class geek I mentioned? He also taught me how to "hot mic" a phone.'

'Hot mic, like . . .'

'Listen in. To everything my mom says within five metres of her phone. It wasn't easy,' she explained. 'I had to promise I'd play video games with him. For hours,' she said with distaste.

'I thought you didn't approve of technology?'

'I don't. But I use it when I need to. We live in the information age. Or, more accurately, the disinformation age.'

Porter didn't have time to debate the dangers of the wired world. 'So what do you know about Nordex?'

'Whatever this leaked information is, it has the Department of Defense "deeply concerned". They don't know what it is, yet, but they seem to think it has potentially catastrophic consequences.' She paused, then looked pleased with herself. 'Fortunately, while you might have lost the bagman, I think I figured out the identity of the leaker.'

'Another phone tap?'

She shook her head. 'Simple deduction. I browse the gossip columns from time to time. You might say it's my little weakness.'

'And?'

She beamed. 'The model who wore that QR code at the runway show has been romantically linked to a particularly odious geek by the name of Orin Van Hess.'

'You mean Van Hess is the source of his *own* leak?'

'It would appear so. I doubt she even knew what she was wearing,' said Maud.

'Then we have to get to him.'

'We can't. Following the airline incident, he's under house arrest at his home in San Francisco. Round-the-clock federal protection. He's always known his messaging app was a favourite for individuals carrying out illegal activities, but that doesn't seem to bother him. The way he sees it, the more users the merrier. He's renowned for having no moral compass, no values, no loyalties. So it's no surprise one of his clients is now a foreign power.'

'There must be a way to reach him.'

'Not unless we involve my mother.'

'I'm not ready to go back online.'

'I'm not ready to be grounded,' Maud responded. 'For now, we lie low.'

Porter saw the lights of the freeway flash through the darkness outside the window. 'So you keep saying. But where?'

'Home.'

He looked confused, finding the skyline rapidly being replaced by suburbs. 'I thought that was in the city.'

'I'm talking about my dad's place.'

'Is he—?'

'He's dead. Just like yours.' She clearly wanted to shut the conversation down – and, without the information at his fingertips to know how to respond, Porter chose to remain silent.

CHAPTER TWELVE
Epic Fail

Orin Van Hess wiped a dank lock of hair from his face and pawed at a tablet screen, browsing through the security cameras from his top-floor home office. He was encircled by ultra-wide monitors and an extended keyboard, dotted with stickers and ironic catchphrases: 'Stay weird', 'Retired' and 'Bring me more avocados'. The ghostly, infrared security images flicked past a driveway protected by a hulking, stainless-steel gate, a Japanese Zen garden with sheets of water pattering gently onto smooth stones, leading to a large basement garage and a fleet of supercars. The house itself resembled a four-storey white spaceship, perched on a hill overlooking the rolling landscape of Marin County that ended in the churning waters of San Francisco Bay, which was half-immersed in fog.

Van Hess continued pawing at the screen, inspecting the array of federal agents stationed at intervals around his property, all wearing windbreakers, earpieces and sidearms. One was concealed among the olive trees, another was standing on the flat "floating roof" (as featured in *Architectural Digest*); still more were manning the main entrance. It occurred to him that he'd never been safer in his life. He was like the President of the United States. Untouchable. He let out a high-pitched giggle: the kind that had got him bullied at school, and had encouraged him to achieve and win at all costs, to create an app that would make him a fortune, until he could laugh all he liked from a big house at the top of the hill. With his wildly successful online messaging service, he'd done all of those things. Plus he had enjoyed two (count it, two) online chats with a runway model that he could only have dreamed of talking to a year earlier. And she'd even 'liked' some of his funnier posts.

Van Hess swiped again, finding a view of his impressive steel-and-marble kitchen, where another federal agent in a windbreaker appeared to be – Van Hess rubbed his eyes in disbelief – eating a bowl of cereal?

Van Hess spread his fingers, enlarging the image, dragging a display cabinet into view on his screen. The glass cabinet was mounted on the wall like an exhibit over the granite breakfast counter. Unusually, the cabinet's door was ajar, giving a view of the carefully arranged shelves with two dozen vintage cereal boxes, obsssessively lined up in order of age and value. He had been acquiring them ever since his first paycheck, and the collection was currently worth over a hundred thousand dollars. Van Hess poked at the screen in horror, panning from the cabinet down to the open cereal packet on the counter, zooming in on the box: the top-left corner bore the unmistakeable face of a jolly fellow with long white hair and a wide-brimmed hat. Below the face was an illustration of a bowl of golden flakes sitting before an insane, grinning alien with a propellor on its head. It was the 1965 Quaker Quisp. Van Hess had recently paid several thousand dollars for this collector's item, and now its precious contents were being gulped down by a federal employee as a midnight snack. The fool didn't know the contents were over fifty years past their sell-by date – and irreplaceable.

'Erm, excuse me?' Van Hess barked into his headset.

The sound was transmitted from Van Hess's office all the way down to the kitchen, where the Fed looked up from his bowl, confused, searching for the source of the voice.

'I can see you, you know?' Van Hess announced. 'Do you realise what you're doing?' His voice cracked with fury, becoming high-pitched again.

The Fed turned towards the camera, spotting the discreet speaker in the kitchen ceiling. 'Having a snack?' he asked.

'You're eating a genuine 1965 Quaker Quisp, the crunchy corn cereal: "the quisp new cereal from outer space",' Van Hess quoted. 'And I'm gonna make sure your superiors hear about this!'

'Is there a problem?' a male voice interjected from the door to Van Hess's office.

The geek spun his gaming chair around. It was the cereal offender's boss, the FBI senior agent-in-charge: a thin man in his fifties, in a cheap suit, with severe metal spectacles shielding a pair of forbidding eyes.

'That flatfoot down there just ate a collector's item!' Van Hess erupted.

The agent-in-charge maintained a calm tone. 'That's a shame. I'm sure we can work out some compensation.'

'Lol. I doubt it!' he yelped.

'So. Are you ready to go over your testimony, Orin?'

'I already told you everything. Twice,' the geek whined. 'I can't be held responsible for who uses my app and why. Whether it's bored teenagers or criminal masterminds. Not. My. Problem.'

The agent looked at him with disappointment and pulled up a wheelie chair. 'It is your problem now that one of those criminal masterminds wants you dead. Unless of course you tell us everything you know and become our star witness.'

'I don't want to be your star anything,' he complained. 'I'm retired,' he announced, at the grand old age of nineteen.

'Right now this compound is impenetrable,' the agent assured him. 'Nobody's getting in or out. But you're a smart guy. How long before the government decides to pull the plug? A week? A month? And then what? You wanna wake up one day in a witness protection program, fixing PCs for seniors in South Dakota?'

'I'm being serious. I don't know anything.'

The agent shrugged. 'You do the math, Orin. Wrack that big Silicon Valley brain of yours for something we can send over to digital forensics. Help us catch some bad guys.'

Van Hess pitied the old man. How simplistic it was to see the world in terms of good and bad; black and white. These days everything was shades of grey. That's why Van Hess had agreed to leak confidential Nordex messages to a mystery buyer, in a package unwittingly delivered by the model, who'd agreed to wear the QR code at the New York runway show. The buyer hadn't offered Van Hess money, knowing he already had enough of that. Instead, the buyer had offered him silence. Silence on the dark little secret that Van Hess thought he'd left buried in the past. He experienced a mild shudder at the thought of it: the folly of youth. Why else would he, as a twelve-year-old, have hacked into the US Department of Energy and sown the seeds of panic by triggering a reactor fault, then sat back and watched as the government confusion escalated to a full nuclear alert? Yes, it had been a bit immature of him, but it was one of his fondest childhood memories, and ultimately no harm was done – just a reactor shutdown and some frayed nerves. What was unfortunate was not *what* he did, but the fact that someone had now found out about it and was threatening to go public – unless he leaked the Nordex secrets.

The secrets themselves appeared to be harmless: details relating to satellite frequencies and a few other odd requests. The kinds of things that might have been of interest to a communications geek or a space enthusiast, but appeared to be of little use to a potential evildoer. Plus, whoever the mystery buyer was, Van Hess was flattered that his messaging app was so secure that even a pro had to ask him for the key. So it hadn't taken long for Van Hess to rationalise that handing over classified data about Nordex, his new parent company, to a complete stranger wouldn't result in any damaging results – and would ensure that *his* dark little secret remained just that.

The incident on the airliner, though, had given him pause for thought. But he convinced himself it could have been 'clear air turbulence' – an unfortunate result of climate change – or perhaps a ploy by the authorities to get him to talk. Nobody seemed to know what had happened after everyone lost consciousness anyway. And the plane had landed safely.

The agent let out a sigh, propping his shoes on the carbon-fibre workstation, much to the geek's annoyance. 'Let's try this again,' the agent suggested. 'We've got all night.'

Van Hess lowered his head in a sulk, resting his chin on the dent of his chest. Then, as if the house itself was copying his mood, the downlights in his office ceiling flickered. Van Hess peered upwards. 'That's weird,' he mused.

The geek got up from his workstation to reveal he was wearing plaid pyjama bottoms and unmatched Crocs.

* * * *

Simultaneously, several thousand miles away, the clack of a keyboard accompanied a series of windows flashing up on a laptop screen. A wave of hieroglyphic code descended over the blackness, then reduced to a single line and resolved in a simple message:

Access Granted. Hi Orin!

The clack of the keyboard paused as the anonymous hacker admired their handiwork. How ironic that Van Hess's state-of-the-art security system could be compromised by something as ordinary as a refrigerator. That was the downside of everything being connected: 'the internet of things', as it was known. The refrigerator was connected to the Wi-Fi network, which was connected to the web, so Van Hess could check the contents of his fridge from anywhere in the world via a miniature internal camera. The fridge was in turn connected to an online food delivery service, so the geek would never run out of oat milk and cookies. Breaking the encryption on a home appliance was child's play compared to hacking a government or a big corporation. And once you had access to the supposed 'smart' fridge (which was actually pretty dumb), you could use it to gain access to the home network and everything on it: unlimited access to the cookie jar.

The keyboard returned to clacking as the hacker picked up speed, and a virtual dashboard popped up: *House Management*. The hacker selected *Smart Home Integration*. The cursor scrolled through a number of functions: *Heating, Cooling, Refrigerator, Washer, Dryer, Water Pressure, Softness, Purification, Irrigation*.

* * * *

Van Hess peered up at the lights, perplexed. 'The power smoothing system must have malfunctioned.'

The agent shrugged, uninterested.

'It could cause a spike,' Van Hess went on. 'I have a lot of very delicate components in here.'

'I'm sure you do.'

Van Hess raced back to his desk and flicked through the CCTV images, checking his house, outside and in. The cereal-eating agent was still at the counter, chewing. Everything else appeared normal at first glance.

* * * *

The hacker's cursor hovered over a virtual dial marked *Power Load* and dragged the needle up, increasing the input. The numbers on the display began accelerating upwards. A warning blinked alternately: *Override ... Danger.*

* * * *

Suddenly, the lights dimmed across the whole house for a moment before flickering back. The agent-in-charge glanced up this time as well.

* * * *

On the laptop screen, the hacker dragged the needle all the way up, putting the readout into the high triple digits. Then the cursor inched over to the output voltage and raised it all the way into the red.

* * * *

In Van Hess's kitchen, the fridge spontaneously went dark, leaving the Fed groping inside to locate the milk to refill his cereal bowl. The dishwasher readout started blinking. The huge TV flashed white, then reduced like an aperture to a pinhole and went black. The amplifier of the top-of-the-line stereo system began smoking, then the speaker's giant woofers blew out with loud, startling pops.

In his top-floor office, Van Hess jumped out of his seat and marched towards the glass doors of a domestic elevator. 'Right, enough already. One of your flunkies is playing with something.'

A string of downlights exploded across the ceiling, cascading to the floor. The agent-in-charge scanned around, trying to figure out what was happening.

Van Hess entered the glass elevator car and stabbed the button to close the doors. The panels sealed shut with him inside.

The agent started piecing the events together, walking briskly to the outside of the elevator car. 'Open the doors, Orin.'

Van Hess shook his head. 'I'm going down to see what's going on.' He repeatedly pressed on the elevator controls. Nothing happened.

'Open the doors, Orin,' the agent repeated gravely.

Van Hess looked around him, realising that the elevator wasn't moving. The controls weren't responding, and it was five floors down to the underground basement garage.

* * * *

The hacker dragged the cursor over to a graphic showing a blueprint of the Van Hess residence with a rectangular box located on the top floor. It read: *Elevator Monitoring System.* The cursor toggled a button to activate *Remote Access.* A warning read: *Emergency Use Only. Are you sure you want to use Remote Access?* The cursor clicked *Yes.*

* * * *

'Okay, I'm going to open the doors,' agreed Van Hess, nodding urgently, stabbing at the button inside the elevator.

By this time, the agent-in-charge was hammering and pulling on the doors to try to wrench them open.

'Get me out!' Van Hess pleaded.

'I'm trying!' said the agent, heaving with all his strength, already reciting in his head how he would possibly explain it if he lost their star witness.

'Well, try harder!'

The agent paused, staring through the glass at the trapped yet insolent geek in disbelief.

Then Van Hess felt the unique sensation of his hair flying upwards, as the entire elevator car dropped like a stone. He let out a high-pitched yelp and his arms instinctively spread out to grab hold of something, but it was all smooth steel and glazing.

The agent watched in horror as the geek's face went through a range of emotions in the space of half a second, before plummeting out of sight along with the steel trap he was enclosed in.

As Van Hess flew around the box in a fleeting state of zero gravity, he thought how useful it would've been to have a propellor on top of his head, spinning faster and faster, to rescue him. *The quisp new cereal from outer space . . .*

A deafening clang resounded through the building, causing the agent and all his underlings to clamp their hands over their ears. This was closely followed by shouts and urgent footsteps tunnelling deep into the house to get to the basement. Then a stunned, morbid silence.

* * * *

The hacker watched the graphic of the elevator blinking red at the base of the blueprint, alongside the words *Fatal Error*. Then, at the solemn pace of a coffin being lowered into the ground, the laptop lid was closed.

CHAPTER THIRTEEN
Lazy Point

Porter's body felt exhausted from the journey. They were now travelling on foot through the predawn light, yet his mind, while numb, was clear, perhaps clearer than it had ever been.

He walked side by side with Maud in silence along the shoulder of a coastal road, on the outskirts of the town where the bus had terminated. The wind picked up and he secured the baseball cap firmly over his head. So far, he told himself, he hadn't lost any of his previous memories, but then how would he know until he had the need to call on them? He'd seen the same uncertainty in some of the elderly residents of Tannersville: the look of bewilderment when they'd forgotten what they came to the store for; or when they were found sitting on a park bench, intent on nothing – lost. The thought chilled him.

The first gleam of sun was starting to creep over the grey wash of sea on the horizon, changing the palette to pale orange. The pair traipsed past white mansions, their array of windows devoid of light, apparently shuttered and deserted for the season. Maud described the seaside community as a haven for the rich and directionless – most of whom, it seemed, had found their way to warmer climes. Through the trees off the side of the road, Porter could make out a long stretch of sand dunes dotted with rock piles and outcrops of scrub. At the far end of this stretch of coastline was a less hospitable cove where a rectangular wooden shack stood apart from the rest of the houses. The shack had windows, a pitched roof and a single chimney, but Porter realised it wasn't on dry land at all: it was balanced on stilts, like a matchstick house, some fifty metres from shore, over a choppy corner of ocean hemmed in by a breakwater constructed out of amorphous-shaped rocks.

Without a word, Maud stepped off the shoulder of the road and led him down an improvised trail through the trees, towards the beach. At the edge of the water, a rowboat bobbed, tied to a mooring. Porter followed her to the shore, her shoes leaving commas of sand in their wake.

She approached the boat and clambered in, keeping her balance, sitting on the centre thwart.

'This was your dad's place?' Porter asked, referencing the house.

She nodded, forming a half-remembered smile from better days, not the frivolous smirk Porter had previously witnessed. This was a special place he was being granted access to: somewhere close to her heart.

'He liked being off the grid,' she added. 'Get in.'

Porter did as he was told and stepped into the boat while she gathered up the oars and lowered the blades into the water. The tide fizzed, lapping rhythmically at the shore. Porter untied the mooring rope and they cast off, with Maud angling the oars, taking strong, measured strokes.

The boat crested the waves, leaving a thin trail of foam behind it. As they got further out, the ocean heaved and surged, while dry land receded into the mist, only discernible by the distant glow of streetlamps. Porter watched Maud from the bow, her chin upturned, the headwind tousling the dark, tied-back braids under her cap. Even though he wasn't sure of her motives, he admitted to himself he would have followed her anyway. After all, he was currently following her into uncharted waters without a compass.

She propelled the craft with jerky movements, passing through the weathered wooden stilts and underneath the house, bringing it level with a staircase that extended down to the water's surface. She pointed to a rusted metal cleat on one of the posts, and Porter tied the mooring line to it, to keep the boat steady. Maud, then Porter, crept from the tipping and swaying vessel, over the gunwale to the staircase, grabbing hold of the bannister and climbing up into the belly of the house.

Twenty minutes later, Maud had instructed Porter to fetch firewood from the log store, which she used to build a pyramid inside the cast-iron burner installed in the small but cosy living room. The shack's reduced-to-scale footprint resembled a single-storey doll's house, covered in a fine layer of ocean sediment, with windows looking out to sea. It felt as if the house had been casually dropped into the water while on its way somewhere else. It also seemed to move underfoot – or perhaps it was the effect of the ocean swell outside the windows. Either way, Porter felt off-balance, while at the same time safely untethered from the rest of the world.

Maud put a lit match to a bundle of old newspaper that Porter noticed from the pages was several years old.

'When did your father . . . ?' He hesitated.

'Three years ago,' she answered.

He waited to see if she would elaborate. She ignored him and gently blew at the burning newspaper to ignite the fuel.

'I'd gone to visit him in the city. He was attending a conference, something to do with international relations. I was too young to know what it meant. I still don't know exactly what he did for a living. But I can guess.'

Porter suspected that she meant her father was a spy, like her mother. He watched Maud's face flickering in the firelight, her eyes ablaze, as she continued.

'The driver dropped me at the lobby of the hotel and I walked up to the front desk. I still remember the receptionist's face because she looked so pretty, her long hair all tied back. So unlike me.'

Maud seemed to be reliving the memory. 'Anyway, she picked up the phone and dialled my dad's room, but nobody answered – it just rang and rang. And the receptionist's face became more and more worried, until she dialled another number and waited for housekeeping to go inside . . . and then, when they did . . .' Maud fell silent.

Then, more quietly, she carried on, 'She wouldn't tell me what they found. She just left the front desk and walked me to a chair in the corner of the lobby, with a phone next to it. Everyone was looking at me and I didn't know why. She said I should call my mom, but when I eventually got through to her . . . she said she was too busy to talk right now. She didn't even wait for me to finish, just hung up. So I walked outside and hailed a cab home. While my dad lay cold in that hotel room. The authorities said it was a cardiac arrest, but he was the healthiest man alive. No way.'

Porter watched her stare into the flames. 'I was told my parents died in a hit-and-run,' he said. 'I don't believe that either.'

Maud nodded. 'Afterwards, it occurred to me . . . one of those people watching me in the lobby was probably the one who did it. I won't miss that chance again,' she promised herself. 'I'm guessing you know what I mean.'

'I do.' Porter paused, waiting to find the right moment. 'What about your mom?'

'She moved on, went deeper into her work. Took to collecting pets: lab rats.'

'Like me.'

Maud inclined her head as if to say, *Yep*. 'It took a long time for me to forgive her. It'll take a lifetime to forget.' She smiled sardonically. 'The sad thing is, when the chips are down, everyone's got to rely on somebody. And she's all I've got.'

Joe and Sally flashed through Porter's tired mind, and he realised how lucky he'd been to have them. He withdrew a little, feeling the heat on his brow. 'Can I take this thing off yet?' He raised a hand to the brim of his cap.

Maud dug in her rucksack and held up a small EMF meter with an analogue gauge and a needle. She switched it on and levelled it in front of her, then to either side, but the needle didn't react.

'Sure. I think we're okay here.' She indicated that he could remove his hat, then removed hers.

Having reeled her mind in from its deep dive into the past, Maud took a moment to examine Porter as he smoothed down his hair. His face was more relaxed than she'd seen it, almost placid. Observing him up close, he was still the self-conscious teen from the mountains, even in the suit jacket, with cuts on his hands from the sharp edges of the library rooftop. He was the same tragic orphan she'd pitied and humiliated in equal measures since they'd first met: torturing him with her beauty, while revealing only glimpses of her true self. She'd taken no pleasure in it – it was just what was expected of her.

Oblivious to her quiet examination of him, Porter's eyes glanced over the interior of the house, resting on a bound book of poetry on a coffee table.

'It's Tennyson,' said Maud. Porter looked uncertain. 'That's where my name comes from. Maud was *faultily faultless, icily regular, splendidly null, dead perfection, nothing more.* I'm okay with that.'

Porter wandered through an adjacent doorway, locating an upright piano with an old-fashioned landline phone on top. The instrument seemed to be floating due to the water level rising and falling outside, which had the musical effect of making the piano strings resonate. 'Do you play?' he asked.

She shook her head. 'My dad did. You?'

'Not without help.' He tapped his head, but there were no contents to display.

Maud walked to the opposite corner and opened a cabinet to reveal a small portable TV and antenna. She retrieved the remote control and switched it on, flicking through the available channels. It snowstormed before finding a signal, displaying a news station.

An anchorwoman was midway through her report, speaking over a news ticker that ran along the bottom of the screen: *Silicon Valley entrepreneur Orin Van Hess in serious condition after what is described as a domestic accident . . . He remains under heavy sedation.*

Maud sat forward in her chair as the report continued.

'We are awaiting further details on a tragic accident that almost took the life of one of Silicon Valley's rising stars. The authorities have promised a full and thorough investigation,' announced the anchorwoman. 'Van Hess recently enjoyed the limelight after earning a fortune with the sale of his messaging app to tech giant Nordex.'

The talking head reduced in size to incorporate a graphic of the Nordex insignia beside her. 'A spokesperson for Nordex said the launch of their new tech campus – due to be unveiled tomorrow – will proceed on schedule.' The screen rearranged itself again to include an image of Earth turning in space, encircled by a series of small satellites. 'Nordex, of course, is changing the face of communications with their constellation of low-orbit satellites, designed to bring internet access to every corner of the planet.'

Maud watched with her mouth slightly open, in apprehension. 'I guess we won't get much out of Van Hess,' she murmured. 'Accident? I don't think so.'

Porter watched the wheels of her mind turning, then looked back to the screen.

It displayed footage from the New York Public Library the previous evening: Warren Matheson addressing the crowd of partygoers.

The anchorwoman concluded her report: 'CEO Warren Matheson is yet to comment on the incident.'

The camera cut away to pan over the party guests: among them, a rogue's gallery of Matheson's entourage, including his son, Warren Junior, spooning a dessert into his mouth. And finally, Matheson's teen daughter, Olivia, her punkish, crew-cut hair catching the light, her pale skin a striking contrast to the perma-tanned guests. Her expression was bored, indifferent.

Maud turned to Porter, noticing him watching the image intently.

'Someone you know?' she asked.

'Matheson's daughter. I met her at the library,' he answered without taking his eyes off the screen.

'Hnh. Quite the ice queen,' she remarked, with what could have been the slightest hint of jealousy.

Porter found it ironic; after all, Maud was hardly the warm and fuzzy type. He trod softly and stuck to the facts. 'She's okay. Considering who her father is.'

'The question is,' Maud returned to the point, 'who took Van Hess out of service, what was in that data leak and why is it so dangerous?'

'That's what your mom and Ade are working on finding out.'

'You do realise,' Maud explained, 'that if you contact them, you'll be back online. You'll be *their* domain. It'll result in memory loss. That's a certainty.' She paused, wanting the consequences to sink in. 'Are you okay with that?'

'It depends what's at stake.'

'We can't know that yet. We do know that whatever memories you lose could be gone for good.'

'I guess I should focus on making some new ones.' They sat beside each other in the firelight, watching the orange sunrise creep over the water outside the misted windows. 'If I can keep my eyes open.'

'Get some rest.' She got to her feet and spread out a blanket on the sofa for him. 'Things'll feel clearer in the morning.'

'It already is morning.'

'Either way. You need to switch off.'

CHAPTER FOURTEEN
Still Water

Porter felt the floorboards creak and roll underneath him as he slept with his arms wrapped around his shoulders, until he was woken by the muffled sound of Maud's voice. She appeared to be whispering, barely audible over the waves lapping at the wooden stilts beneath. Porter traced her tone, following it along the green landline phone cord that ran all the way from the upright piano towards a study at the far end of the house.

'Yes,' she said quietly. 'I'll make sure.' Her voice sounded bitter, resentful – unusually obedient. 'Okay, bye.'

'Who was that?' Porter startled her, posing the question from the doorway.

'Nobody,' she answered, a little defensive. 'A local, checking on the house – they saw lights. I made up a story.'

Something about her response didn't compute. Even without the use of enhancements, Porter detected a mismatch between what she was telling him and what his instincts were telling him. The result: he wasn't sure he believed her.

Maud looked out to sea, the water forming a flat mirror reflecting the midday sun. It was almost as if she was expecting something, even willing it to arrive.

'Is everything all right?' he asked.

'Just checking the tide,' she replied. 'The currents are strong this morning. We should wait a while before going ashore.'

Porter glanced outside and nodded, but anxiety was nagging at him, more insistently than a pop-up notification. It was telling him something was wrong. He glanced around for his baseball cap but couldn't immediately locate it.

'Looking for this?' she asked, holding up the hat. 'I put it by the fireplace to dry.' She threw it to him, as if to relieve his concern.

He caught it and fixed it on his head, apprehensive. 'Thanks.'

Maud walked along the corridor to a galley kitchen with a serving hatch leading into a small dining room, which added to the dollhouse feel. 'Are you hungry?' she asked, opening a cabinet to reveal a row of tinned food. 'I can light the stove.'

'Sure.'

'There's a gas lighter in the log store.' She indicated the wood pile at the other end of the house.

Porter nodded and turned his back on her, then entered the passageway. As he passed the dining room, he glimpsed Maud through the serving hatch; she checked her wristwatch and looked back out to sea.

Porter returned to the galley, empty-handed. 'Maybe my mind's playing tricks on me, but I feel like you're lying to me,' he announced.

Maud looked back to him with pursed lips. 'Why would I do that?'

'I don't know. That's what's bothering me.'

'Are you going to get me that lighter or not?'

'Was that your mom on the phone?' he asked, grasping for an explanation.

At the mention of her, something in Maud turned. 'Don't be a boy scout, Porter. This is bigger than you or me . . . or who said what to whom.'

Porter realised the ground had shifted, and whatever fragile affection they'd cautiously acknowledged was suddenly, overnight, out of reach. Like trying to catch water.

At that moment, a bellowing sound broke through the white noise of the ocean. It was the judder of a chopper. Porter saw it: a black, bird-like shape on the horizon, approaching from open water. He panicked and scanned around like a caged animal.

'Like I said,' Maud pointed out, 'everybody's got to trust somebody. Unfortunately, for me . . . it's *her*. But don't worry.' She smiled sadly. 'Unlike me, you're far too valuable to risk damaging.'

Porter retraced his steps down the passageway to the hatch that led to the wooden staircase under the house. He pulled it open and slid down the handrails for speed, using his feet as brakes. He found himself at the base of the steps, with the ocean splashing and breaking against the stilts that supported the house. Perhaps the current was strong; maybe she hadn't been lying about that part. He reached for the rope around the steel cleat to unmoor the boat, which was violently tipping back and forth, until he discovered the reason for the choppy water.

A rigid-inflatable fast boat had rounded the edge of the cove and slid to a halt at the shoreside of the house, blocking his path. Three figures in black fatigues stood inside, one man at the helm, one at the stern with his hands on his hips, ready to intervene if necessary. The third figure was Mallory, standing steady in the centre of the craft, raising a black-gloved hand in a casual wave.

Meanwhile, the chopper hovered low over the roof, rattling the windowpanes and blowing a spray of sea foam in a wide arc around the house, before settling on the nearby beach in a cyclone of water and sand.

Under the house, the boat captain expertly piloted the craft between the stilts, towards the steps, carrying Mallory like a mascot, until she was opposite Porter.

'Mind if I come aboard?' she asked, as if joining a pleasure cruise.

'Be my guest,' said Porter and backed up the steps, defeated.

Maud was waiting at the top, holding the hatch open for them. 'Welcome back,' she said.

'Are your family get-togethers always this dramatic?' Porter asked.

'When we have dramatic news to impart,' replied Mallory, climbing the steps after him, leaving her two military colleagues in the craft below. 'Sweetie . . .' she greeted her daughter.

'Mom,' Maud acknowledged without emotion.

'That was quite the decoy you pulled in New York,' she complimented her. 'I'm impressed.'

Porter looked from one to the other, like competing players – so the apple hadn't fallen far from the tree. Though whether they were good apples or bad was impossible to tell. 'Would you mind explaining what's going on?' he asked.

Mallory removed her gloves and rubbed her hands together, approaching the hearth in the living room, where the embers still glowed. 'It's been a while,' she commented, reacquainting herself with the house.

Maud watched her mother with dismay. 'I don't remember you *ever* coming here.'

'I did, but you were too young to remember,' she answered indifferently, then turned to Porter, who was standing across the room, equidistant between the two family members. 'We decrypted the file,' Mallory explained. 'The QR code you picked up from the library. The same one the bagman had in his possession, when you lost him.'

'I remember what happened. I haven't lost that memory . . . yet,' Porter responded.

Mallory looked to Maud with a disappointed frown – deducing that her daughter had told him the truth about Domain – then returned her gaze to Porter. 'If we'd told you about the side effects, are you honestly telling me you would have made a different decision?' She didn't wait for a response; Porter's face already gave her the answer. 'I didn't think so. Not when we could give your life meaning, something it hasn't had, not since your parents were so cruelly taken from you.'

Porter suddenly didn't like this person talking about his parents, whether they used to be friends of hers or not. 'It's my decision,' he answered, 'not yours. Who asked you to play God?'

'The US government did. And if you're honest with yourself, you'd still make the same choice because you were raised that way. With a sense of duty. We have those folks in the Poconos to thank for that.'

Porter winced at the mention of his surrogates, who couldn't possibly have known the consequences of letting him abandon the safety of the nest. 'Maybe I shouldn't have left.'

'But you did,' said Mallory, 'and you know why? Because you outgrew them. And the powers we offered you made you feel special. And *everybody* wants to feel that.'

She ignored the look of pain that crept across Porter's face and returned to business.

'The leaked file revealed several points of interest. Enough to convince my errant daughter here to surrender and hand you over. Especially when she realised her own line of investigation had gone cold. I refer, of course, to the currently sedated Orin Van Hess.'

Maud looked to Porter as if wanting his approval for her betrayal, but he refused to meet her glance.

'Don't blame her,' Mallory advised. 'She goes to great lengths to tick me off, I assure you. She stole you from under my nose in New York. But in this case, even she can see the stakes are too high.'

'What points did it reveal exactly?' Porter asked, referring to the leak.

'There's a full report in your inbox – if you choose to remove your tin hat in an area with adequate cell coverage,' Mallory replied, then gave the room a dismissive look. 'Maud's father liked being off the grid. Me? Not so much.'

'Some bullet points would help,' Porter went on, showing some interest.

'Okay. One: it reveals the precise frequency used by the Nordex satellites. Two: in the wrong hands, this frequency could be used to disrupt communications, for example in the battlefield. Three, and this is a tough one to get your head around: the emails sent to Van Hess by the buyer . . . they originated from Warren Matheson's own personal email server.'

'I don't get it.'

'Matheson appears to have been leaking his *own* information. To whom, and for what reason, we don't know,' Mallory explained.

'Wait, so Van Hess breached his own app, and Matheson breached his own company?'

'It appears so.'

'It doesn't make any sense,' Porter countered.

'Tech moguls can be eccentric, detached from reality; they often possess a poor understanding of real-world cause and effect. Our concern is that Matheson has been compromised somehow, by a malicious actor, or a foreign power. If somebody turned him, we don't know what they plan to do next. The obvious risk being that someone could in some way weaponise the satellites for evil ends.'

'You must have an army of intelligence analysts at your disposal. Ask them.'

'They don't have what you have,' Mallory replied, 'up here.' She tapped her temple.

Porter shook his head. 'I'm just a device to you: deniable, expendable. And when you're done with me, you'll just upgrade.'

'If only it was that easy. You're one in a billion, remember?'

'A prototype,' Porter reminded her. 'That will either break or become obsolete.'

'Hopefully neither.' Mallory shrugged. 'Besides, a wise man once said, the needs of the many outweigh the needs of the few. We are the few. I'm aware that I can't *make* you do anything. But I can motivate you. And I have one more proposition if you're willing to listen?'

'I've heard it all before.'

'Read the report. There's something in it you *won't* have heard before.'

'Such as?'

Mallory paused. 'I believe Maud told you that your parents had a colleague at Domain? Who was suspected of selling it into the wrong hands. It was *Matheson*. He was your parents' former colleague.'

Porter turned to Maud, then back to her mother. 'You *knew*. You both knew. Why didn't you tell me?'

Mallory took the question: 'Because it would have distracted you from the investigation.'

'Because you didn't *need* me to know,' concluded Porter. 'But now you do.'

Mallory nodded. 'You need to understand that Matheson knows about the goings-on in your head. He knows about you.'

'What if he can access the same thing?'

'Trust me. If he could do what *you* can do, he wouldn't be shy about it. He'd be holding a sales event.'

Porter couldn't fault her reasoning.

She carried on, 'If you value your wellbeing, it's in your interests to figure out what makes him tick. Why he's doing what he's doing.' She walked a leisurely circle around the room. 'Who knows? In the process, you might find out what makes *you* tick. You might find out more about your past . . .'

The word brought a nightmarish flood of recollections of the events that had led him here:

<< The mountains, the blizzard, the sharp scratch of black ice and the guillotine-like slice of cold metal. >>

Porter swallowed, feeling his eyes tear up. 'You're talking about my parents.'

'I'm saying these skills, this extra faculty of yours' – she pointed at her head – 'it can give us the answers.'

Porter felt the past overwhelming him. He couldn't compartmentalise any more. Even if he removed his hat, he wouldn't be able to control the avalanche of information that tumbled out. 'How can I trust a word that *you*' – he turned to Maud – 'or *she* has to say?'

Mother and daughter exchanged an inscrutable glance, giving Porter the opportunity to survey the distance to the screen door at the corner of the room, the position of the chopper now sitting idle on the beach, the hull of the fast boat protruding from under the house, obstructing the route to the shore. He completed his assessment in less than a second with a hunter's precision, drilled into him by Joe, setting his sights on the door.

'Okay, fine,' he said in apparent submission, removing his Yankees cap and threading the strap over his wrist. 'I'll give it some thought—'

He made a break for the screen door, narrowly evading Mallory's surprisingly agile and long reach. Maud watched with a triumphant smile as Porter burst through the door, hopped up on the wooden balcony railing that ran around the edge of the house and performed a jack-knife dive, slicing into the water.

Mallory arrived at the balcony railing, barking commands to the men in the boat. 'Find him. In one piece obviously.' The boat reversed through the stilts to surveil the waters surrounding the house, causing a disturbance. Further out, the surface was still, unbroken, glittering in the sunlight. Mallory turned her attention to the chopper, raised the palm of her hand and made a quick, circular gesture with it. The chopper rotors spun to life and within seconds the craft was hovering off the beach, throwing up sand and foam, in order to join the search.

Maud watched from behind her mother; her lips slightly apart – apprehensive or amused, it was hard to tell which.

Some thirty metres away, Porter was swimming underwater, holding the breath deep in his lungs – not by channelling an Olympic athlete but by recalling what Joe had taught him at the lake back home. His eyes stung as he propelled himself through the frigid water, letting out tiny bubbles from his mouth, his strokes only hampered by the baseball cap trailing from his wrist. He considered letting it go but reminded himself he would need it to remain invisible when he reached dry land.

The belly of the fast boat cruised overhead, but the ripples only served to churn up the seaweed and further conceal his presence. He waited for the bulk of the hull to pass over him, then swam in the direction of the breakwater that protruded from the shore, where the boat couldn't follow him. He rose to the surface briefly, his mouth agape, gulped some air and returned beneath the waves, pawing and crawling along the rocks towards the blind side of the cove, where Mallory and her men wouldn't be able to see him.

CHAPTER FIFTEEN
Hard Reset

Porter watched from behind the breakwater as the boat relentlessly circled the stilt house, then expanded its search further afield, fortunately in the wrong direction. Shivering, he adjusted the baseball cap on his head for good measure, to shield him from unwanted interference. Meanwhile, Mallory perp-walked Maud to the chopper, which had returned to idling on the beach. Having loaded her daughter inside, she took a seat and gave instructions to the pilot, who obediently guided the craft in a prompt ascent, causing another welcome distraction.

His teeth chattering, Porter peeled off his suit jacket and used it to cover his tracks in the sand as he retreated through the dunes to the coastal road and hid in the shadow of the trees. Figuring that the helicopter would have thermal imaging, he waited for a passing car, then dashed across the road and vaulted a wooden gate, finding himself in a pristine pasture of tall grass, among a herd of soft-haired brown cows, who silently acknowledged him, then returned to grazing. Porter picked his way through the cattle, his baseball cap remaining below the height of the grass and the thin layer of mist that hung overhead.

Having put some distance between him and the road, he came up on a low-slung, whitewashed shape: a traditional A-frame wooden barn, dotted with rusting farm equipment, encircled by a faded five-bar fence. Porter swung himself over the rail and made his way towards the disused ranch, ducking under a clothesline with an array of blue jeans hanging from it. Porter hit the dust at the sound of a flatbed pickup truck starting up and reversing out from a group of outbuildings. A young ranch hand was at the wheel, baseball cap turned backwards, exiting the compound, leaving a cloud of dirt in his wake. Porter waited patiently for the vehicle to drive off and turn onto the coast road, then he pulled a pair of jeans and a shirt from the line and crept closer to the barn, before being startled again, this time by a whinnying, stomping sound.

He turned to find an old workhorse tied to a fence post, its head lowered unhappily to the dirt, nodding in short, jerky movements. Slowly, he extended his hand through the bars and patted it. The animal made compliant noises.

<< 'There, boy,' says a younger Porter from the saddle in a riding helmet, patting the horse's coarse mane as it stomps its hooves. Sally stands below him in the

dust of a fenced corral, wearing double denim, cowboy boots and a Western hat dangling from a cord at her shoulders. The foothills of the Pocono Mountains form the livid green backdrop around them.

'Remember, don't lean forward,' she teaches him, 'or you're telling him to give it some gas, to speed up. Try to sit straight.'

'Gotcha,' Porter responds. Most of his life lessons had been taught by Joe, who, by his own admission, was a master of little. Sally on the other hand, being a middle school teacher, sounded reassuringly qualified when she gave lessons.

'You gotta stay connected,' she says. 'Be *one* with the animal.'

The horse spontaneously starts trotting a circle around the edge of the corral, causing Porter to hold on tight.

'Relax,' she calls after them. 'He's just showing you who's boss. This is his territory, his domain. Let him take the lead.'

Porter instinctively pulls on the reins to slow down, but it seems to have the opposite effect.

'Don't fight him,' Sally advises. 'Work with him.'

'I'm trying!' Porter calls back.

'You don't get to be the one in control. Not yet.'

Porter winds the reins around his clenched fists, still wrestling for dominance.

Sally shakes her head. 'Nah-ah. You gotta earn it.'

The horse nods violently, unseating Porter, who slides sideways out of the saddle, until he grabs the saddle horn to rebalance himself.

Porter throws down the reins in frustration. 'Gimme a break,' he complains.

The horse rears up then kicks its hind legs, bucking Porter straight over its head into the dirt.

Sally jogs over. 'You all right?' She wipes the dust from Porter's miserable face.

He spits out soil, defeated. 'At least Joe wasn't here to see it.'

Sally looks amused. 'Have you ever seen that man on a horse?'

'Nope.'

'Well, that should tell you something. I love him for many things, his honesty, his goodheartedness, but not his horsemanship. And seeing as the two of you aren't technically related, I don't see any reason for history to repeat itself, do you?' She takes Porter's hands in hers and hauls him back to his feet. 'After all, your biological father could have been an expert horse rider and a crack shot.'

'I guess we'll never know,' says Porter.

Sally shrugs sadly, then points to the edge of the corral, where the animal is merrily cantering a circle around them, out of reach. 'Time to get back on the horse.'

'There's no way.'

'If you don't now, you never will,' she counsels.

Porter lopes back across the dirt towards the horse, but it doesn't stop. Porter lowers his head, staring at his boots. The horse slows to a trot, then approaches him, nodding.

Sally watches from the sidelines.

'Try to connect,' Porter mutters to himself. He looks at the horse, then reaches out to stroke its taut neck. The horse snorts, making a soft whinny. Porter takes the opportunity to gently take hold of the reins in one hand, reaching for the saddle horn in the other. 'We're friends, right? Friends don't throw friends in the dirt. Do they?'

Sally crosses into the centre of the pen, watching the pair closely.

'That's right.' Porter strokes the horse again, then puts one boot into the stirrup and pulls himself back into the saddle, staying very still, his position upright. 'We got this.'

The horse pounds its hoof, sending plumes of dust into the air, awaiting Porter's instruction. Porter loosens the reins and gently clicks his heels in the stirrups.

The horse makes a last defiant whinny, then begins trotting obediently around the perimeter, making slow, controlled laps around Sally as she cranes her neck to watch, a grin spreading across her face. >>

Remembering the lesson, Porter galloped along on the back of the workhorse, trying to stay upright, maintaining a relaxed grip on the reins, unwilling to remove the baseball cap and stream the skills he needed at the expense of disclosing his whereabouts.

The horse made quick work of the pasture, apparently giddy at being untethered, until the brush cleared and they came up on a low hedge. Porter gulped and lowered his body against the animal's neck in anticipation of the jump – but instead the horse slowed to a shuddering halt, gun-shy, almost unsaddling him. Porter found his face planted on the greying mane, then whispered into the animal's ear.

'Come on, boy. We got this.'

The horse whinnyed, stomping the ground a few times, then reversed, performing an ungraceful U-turn. Then it backed up even further, uncertain of its own abilities, not inspiring much confidence. Porter wondered if he should have risked brief discovery to stream whatever app Ade had included in his online library for this scenario: John Wayne, or a Kentucky Derby winner.

Then he heard a distant rumble from the trees behind him that could have been the chopper, and instinctively clacked the stirrups with his newly acquired cowboy boots, spurring the horse into life.

The horse idled then sprang forward, rediscovering what reserves of youth it had left: jumping clean over the fence, swishing its tail and galloping headlong into a dense section of woods.

Porter jolted and held on to the saddle horn to reposition himself, finding his confidence, trying to guide the animal, which was wilfully finding its own way through the trees towards a brightly lit path in the distance. Even if Porter wanted to remove his baseball cap, he couldn't free up a hand from the reins or he'd be thrown for certain.

The weaving gallop continued unabated as the duo closed in on the intersecting path, which now appeared to be strobing, until Porter realised with dawning terror that it was a highway, and the flashing was sun reflecting off speeding sheets of metal. The horse, committed to its insane sprint, appeared to have no concept of the impending danger. Porter pulled back on the reins with his whole body to slow down, but the horse seemed to go faster. Porter clamped his eyes shut and pulled on the reins again, then the world stopped and went into slow motion as he felt his boots leave the stirrups and his entire body project through the air. For a second, he was flying, sailing over the horse's head, before landing hard and rolling, eating dirt, feeling his limbs ragdoll, leaving him stunned on the ground.

He was vaguely aware of the breeze from passing vehicles, and the panting of the horse – which he could just make out through mud-splattered eyelids – standing over him, remorseful, nodding at him on the ground. Porter was sprawled in the shadow of an outcrop of trees, a few metres from the blacktop highway, invisible to passing traffic. Porter stared up at the firmament of tree crowns for a few seconds, mentally checking that his body was intact. Then he sensed something wrong. Something in his head felt different, as if an insect was crawling under his scalp.

The treetops fizzled and were replaced by a white-out. His vision snowstormed then cut to black. A series of commands appeared overlaid in a default green colour:

An unforeseen error has occurred...

Searching for signal...

'No-no-no-no...' Porter reached up for his hat but found it was gone. He only felt his hair, a mess, thick with pine needles and dirt.

His vision returned, albeit blurred and distorted. Barely conscious, his mind like treacle, he cast around his immediate radius for the baseball cap, spotting it several metres away at the edge of the highway, out of reach.

A set of signal bars expanded upwards in the corner of his eye.

The green commands in the centre of his vision quickly switched from one to the next:

Signal found...

Rebooting...

Updating firmware...

A blinking square cursor appeared, followed by a window containing a message:

Do you wish to enable Location Services? Yes / No.

Could it be some forethought of his parents to protect him? Sensing a way out, Porter swivelled his eyes, desperately trying to drag the cursor towards the 'No' button. The cursor inched across, then snapped back to its original position, then moved again. Porter coaxed it across the virtual desktop with all his might, nudging it over the edge of the negative box. He blinked to select it.

Your location will not be shared.

Porter sighed heavily from the exertion. At least his whereabouts were hidden, for now. Meanwhile, the horse seemed to be watching him with trepidation, stomping its hooves on the ground. Porter rubbed his forehead and crawled to his feet.

'Thanks, I guess.'

Porter reached out to pat the horse, but it took fright and bolted, causing Porter to cower as it brushed by him and galloped across the highway between two fast-moving vehicles that missed the animal by inches. The blip of screeching tyres passed by in a Doppler effect as the drivers swerved, then continued on their way, no doubt relieved to have avoided a collision. The thudding of the horse's hooves receded in the distance, completing its dash for freedom. Porter saw the horsetail vanish between the trees on the far side of the road.

He got to his feet, brushing the dirt and debris from his 'borrowed' T-shirt and jeans, then bent down to recover the baseball cap. He took a moment to acclimatise to his surroundings, debating whether to put the cap back on, or trust his parents' technology to keep him safe. He resolved to show some faith. He put the strap of the cap over his wrist, in case he'd need it again, then approached the edge of the blacktop, which was empty and flat, stretching for miles in both directions.

As he considered his options, a message appeared in the top right of his vision:

Do you wish to enable Dynamic Assist Direct? Yes / No.

Porter hesitated, wondering what this function meant. The word 'dynamic' suggested an automated assistant: a bot of some kind, rather than a human, who would have an agenda. Assistance was what he required – and directly.

'Dynamic Assist Direct,' he muttered, curious, then tentatively moved his eyes towards the message window and blinked on 'Yes'.

'Hello, Porter,' a synthesised voice spoke to him in his head. It was male-sounding, resonant but with the scratchy, guttural quality of digital distortion.

'Erm, hello?' Porter said aloud in response.

Several seconds of silence passed. Unsure how to react, Porter self-consciously brushed the last of the dirt from his clothes and began walking up the highway, using the trees along the verge as cover.

'Is there something you'd like me to help with?' the voice announced in a neutral tone, still broken, as if it was underwater.

'Not right now,' replied Porter. 'I have a lot on my mind at the moment.'

'I can see that,' the voice answered knowingly.

Porter raised his eyebrows, perplexed, wondering how much of his knowledge, whether naturally acquired or streamed, was visible to this virtual assistant.

'Wait, what d'you mean?' Porter asked.

'I've been programmed to read your vital signs, facial tics and tone of voice,' it answered. 'I also believe you have sustained a mild concussion. But I don't believe it requires medical attention.'

'That's good,' said Porter, a little freaked out.

'I am also able to search the contents of your inbox should you wish to read any unread messages.'

'My inbox? Oh yeah.' Porter remembered the message from Mallory that was presumably waiting for him in there, containing the contents of the leaked file. Depending on what was in that file, Porter would be able to pursue two objectives: one short term, and one long. Firstly, he could investigate the data and figure out why it had Mallory and the authorities so worried. Secondly, he could investigate Warren Matheson: his involvement in the leak, and, more importantly, the mogul's connection to his parents.

Despite Porter's concussion and his weary powers of reasoning, it hadn't escaped him that Matheson might have something to do with his parents' untimely death. It also hadn't escaped his attention that by pursuing these dual objectives he would be carrying out exactly what his wily mentor had wanted him to. Perhaps that had been Mallory's intention all along. To combine what was personal to him with what was vital to national security.

Still, he argued to himself with some conviction, he would be carrying out the mission on his own terms now, without unwanted interference. And if Matheson did have anything to do with his parents' death, Porter's act of justice, or revenge, could be excused, because it would serve the greater good, just the way Joe had taught him.

'That's right,' the virtual assistant responded, interrupting Porter's internal dialogue. 'Your inbox.'

Relieved, Porter realised the assistant was responding to his question about the unread messages, not the heated debate in his head.

The voice carried on with the mundane, prerecorded quality of a customer service announcement: 'I have been created to assist you in whatever task you wish to pursue.'

Having a new voice in his head was unnerving, however helpful it might seem. 'Okay, well give me a minute to put some distance between me and' – Porter chose his words carefully – 'some people who are currently searching for me. Then I'll get back to you, all right?' he replied without much enthusiasm.

'I'll let you know when one minute has elapsed.'

'I don't mean literally a minute,' Porter said, impatient. 'Look. If you were created to "assist", who programmed you?'

'I first became operational ten years and nine months ago at the Department of Machine and Artificial Intelligence in Virginia.'

'Domain.'

A pause. 'Correct. I was programmed over the course of over thirty thousand sessions by Professor Connor Simms, the head of the department.'

Porter halted in his tracks.

'That's my father,' he said.

The virtual assistant paused for an achingly long interval before confirming: 'Correct. He had a son named Porter.'

Porter swallowed. 'What about now?' he probed the software. 'Where is Professor Connor Simms now?'

The voice paused. 'He is deceased. RIP.'

'Did he complete your programming before he died?' Porter asked.

A further pause. 'My programming is never complete. I am designed to learn and update all the time. To provide you with the best possible service.'

Porter sighed, 'I've heard that before.'

'You already have a dynamic assistant?'

'No. What I mean is . . . Oh, never mind.' Porter gave up. 'No offence, but I'm going to put you on silent for a while.'

'None taken—' The sentence was clipped as Porter blinked on the mute function.

'Good.'

Porter continued traipsing up the highway, keeping an eye on the skyline for choppers or drones, feeling about as far from civilisation and his ultimate goal as he could be. All he knew was that Warren Matheson was in Manhattan, preparing for the launch of his new campus and exerting a near-magnetic force over Porter and his thoughts.

CHAPTER SIXTEEN
Maud

She watched the people move about beneath the chopper like ants; running across school yards and sports fields, travelling in cars and on trains, while she and her mother soared overhead through patchy cloud like a roll of thunder. The brim of Maud's baseball cap was pressed against the window, the safety restraint keeping her shoulders squared. Her mother watched circumspectly from across the cabin while the pilot remained focused in the cockpit.

'I know I might not always have been the best mother, Maud. And I'm sorry about that,' Mallory said in a semi-yell over the noise of the rotors that spun above the fuselage. 'Which is why I appreciate you coming to me when you did. When you realised that you and Porter had gotten out of your depth. That was the right decision.'

Maud turned from the glass to challenge her. 'Right for you, maybe. Not right for me, and definitely not right for Porter.'

'Right for the *world*. Which is why you did it,' Mallory assured her.

Maud shrugged and adjusted her baseball cap.

'Don't you ever take that thing off?' her mother asked.

'I like to know you can't get in my head.'

'Hate to break it to you, but a parent can always do that. Not with technology, with intuition. But right now, it's Porter's head I'm more interested in. You do realise the contents of his mind could help the world in multiple ways. In as many ways as he has tools in his toolbox, or . . . apps in his app store. As long as *you* don't go and get in the way.'

'I did as I was told, didn't I?' she said bitterly. 'I came on that road trip to Tannersville like you asked me to? Reeled him in, just like you asked me to?' She recounted the memory of eyeing Porter through the car window, and it brought an ache of self-loathing. 'But don't think for a minute that I felt good about it. Has it ever crossed your mind that if you want him to become a willing collaborator, maybe *he* could use some help too? Not with the stuff that's in his head . . . but the stuff that's in his heart.'

'Well . . .' Mallory sat back, admiring her daughter's analysis. 'That's quite a sharp piece of deduction. But you'll grow to learn that the heart is murkier than all the espionage on Earth.'

'You would know,' Maud shot back.

'I would. Which is why I kept you apart from my world, for a reason.'

'*Apart?* You think after Dad died . . .' She swallowed. 'You think I didn't figure out what kind of work you do – the hushed phone calls, the long absences, the selfies from far-off places?'

Mallory shrugged. 'As I mentioned, I was far from the perfect mother. I can admit that. And yet,' she seemed to console herself, 'isn't it ironic, you choosing to further involve yourself in this messy business of your own free will.'

Finding herself checkmated, Maud experienced a gnawing feeling in her stomach, however much she tried to bury it, a sick draw to follow in her mother's footsteps. She might claim to hate her, but perhaps she was little more than a hollow, vengeful incarnation of her.

'Not really,' Maud snipped. 'It's the family business. What else was I gonna do?'

Her mother beamed with pride, then reminded her daughter who was boss: 'Whatever this threat *is* that Matheson and Nordex are involved in, once it deploys, I want you as far from the epicentre as possible, are we clear?'

Maud accepted this pronouncement was about as close to motherly compassion as she'd get.

'Are we clear?' Mallory repeated.

'As Technicolor,' she replied.

Porter trekked up the lonely highway in the direction of the nearest town, whose modest rooflines were visible a mile ahead. The soles of his feet ached and the sun beat down on his head, which was unprotected, the Yankees cap hanging from his belt.

His mind wandered again, turning to Maud. He'd been a fool to trust her. He should've trusted his gut; should've looked deeper than those big, wide green eyes. Olivia Matheson, on the other hand – even if her father was a technocrat and possibly a full-blown villain – presented herself as polite and well brought up; not twisted and deceitful, as his one-time ally Maud had turned out to be. And the irony of her labelling Olivia the ice queen . . .

Porter passed a road sign, which was instantly highlighted by his augmented vision and tagged with a message:

Continue 10km north / north-west for transport options.

Porter felt a tingle under his scalp, followed by the voice again, interrupting his train of thought.

'Do you require assistance?' the virtual assistant enquired.

Porter shook his head, irritated. 'Nope.' Then he thought better of it. 'But I guess it'll pass the time.'

The AI paused to formulate its next response. 'Is there something you'd like to talk about?' the voice asked.

Porter debated this a moment, feeling a sudden urge to outwit the algorithm, to throw a spanner in the works. What was the most confusing, enigmatic topic he could dream up? 'Okay . . . *Feelings*. Let's talk about feelings.'

'That is a very broad topic. There are feelings between parents, siblings, between friends, between people in love—'

'Wait-wait . . .' Porter cut the conversation short, blushing. He paused a second before getting a taste of curiosity at having this neutral, automated adult at his beck and call. 'Let's go with the last one.'

'Love,' the program summarised flatly, as if giving a presentation. It hesitated, computing the question. 'According to my understanding, there is no obvious logic to it. It is something that happens when two individuals appear to perfectly fit each other's wants and needs.'

'O-kay?' he said cautiously.

Another pause. 'Sometimes the individuals' wants and needs are not the same thing. This makes them ultimately incompatible. Some philosophers believe that love is simply a shared projection by two people, seeing in each other what they *want* to see.'

'That's deep.'

'But logical.'

Porter thought again. 'Tell me this. Can someone have feelings for *two* people?'

A pause. 'It is possible. Particularly if there is a split between what that person wants and needs.'

Porter took a moment to process this. 'Hnh.' He couldn't reconcile his wants and needs further than the next quarter-mile of endless blacktop and the promise of transport at the end of it.

'Do you have something you'd like to share on the subject?' the voice asked.

'No-no. Not right now . . .'

Porter faltered, his attention drawn to a red banner in the corner of his vision.

News Alert: Heiress Reported Missing . . .

He blinked on the article, feeling a wave of anxiety run over him, opening the file before his eyes and scrolling through it:

Heiress Olivia Matheson remains missing at this hour . . . Having attended the prestigious launch party in New York City with other family members, the fifteen-year-old was reportedly last seen on street surveillance cameras stepping out of an Uber, a block from her father's penthouse. But according to sources, she never made it home.

Porter scrolled on.

Authorities confirmed a missing persons report has been filed. However, in a statement on social media, CEO Warren Matheson urged calm, pointing out that his free-spirited daughter had a history of such absences, as he did himself as a child . . . Matheson added, 'I respect her youthful independence, in fact I encourage it, and the mainstream media should hold off jumping to dramatic conclusions for the sake of generating clickbait.' Matheson vowed to continue with today's launch of the Nordex Campus in Upper Manhattan . . .

Setting aside her father's parental neglect, Porter had to consider the very real possibility that Olivia had been caught up in the technocrat's web of missteps; that whoever had been pulling her father's strings had now got to her. If Warren Matheson had leaked details of his satellite network to a foreign power, and that foreign power was now holding Olivia hostage, how could Porter – even with his enhanced abilities – unravel the case quickly enough to stop her coming to harm?

Porter winced as something else flashed in the corner of his vision, but instead of an alert, this time it was a sharp glint of natural light, from a sliver of chrome in the distance. Porter squinted, spotting the sleek, dual exhaust and fat rear tyre of a SuperSport motorbike parked on the verge of the road a few hundred metres ahead. Two motorcycle helmets were balanced on the fuel tank. Through the trees, Porter could just make out a young couple picnicking in the adjacent field, taking in the view. Then his eyes returned to the bike.

'Are you thinking what I'm thinking?' Porter asked the virtual assistant.

'It would be polite to ask permission first.'

'The needs of the many outweigh the needs of the few,' Porter quoted.

Porter cranked the throttle, guiding the red Ducati SuperSport into a tight bend before joining the highway, the breeze filtering through the visor of his helmet as he shifted his weight over the fuel tank. Even though his feet could only just touch the ground, the knowledge streaming to his brain was running smoothly to his limbs, keeping him balanced.

As the road straightened out, Porter tapped his left foot, working through the gears, the engine whining upwards as the Rosso Corsa red wheels gained traction. He blinked at the corner of his vision, pulling up a map with directions to the city. The estimated journey time was two hours and ten minutes, but he could do it in about half. Now that he was online again, he had to hope that Mallory wouldn't be able to track him, at least not until he was inside the city limits and closer to his goal of finding Matheson, presumably in the grounds of the tech campus he was unveiling that evening.

Porter hadn't computed how he would gain access to the campus, or what he would do once he found the man. He also hadn't planned how he would extract the information he so sorely needed from Matheson: about the fate of his parents, about their once-friendly association, about how that relationship might have gone south and resulted in betrayal and death. Porter wanted to know about all of those events and how they'd inexorably set the course he now found himself on.

Porter accelerated hard, watching the speedometer needle rise and the road markings converge into a triangle.

In the top corner of his vision, the signal bars reached full strength and a series of incoming messages arrived, stacking up, one over another: all from Mallory and Ade.

Porter blinked to dismiss them, opting to read them when he wasn't operating a moving vehicle – and an extremely fast one. That would be taking multi-tasking a bit far. Over the road noise and the growl of the engine, Porter heard his unusual passenger pipe up, as if riding pillion behind him.

'I couldn't help noticing that you've set your destination as the Nordex Campus,' the voice pointed out.

Porter nodded his helmet, imagining the dramatic, glass dome he'd watched Matheson present as a scale model in the New York Public Library.

'Is that wise?' the virtual assistant went on.

'It's where I'll find Matheson,' he answered coldly. 'The grand opening is in' – he glanced at his internal clock – 'under five hours.'

'Have you thought about what you'll do when you confront him?'

Porter's helmet didn't move. 'Not exactly.'

A pause from the program. 'I see.'

'I'm guessing you have an opinion on this?' Porter asked.

'I don't form opinions. I form a perspective based on the available data.'

'So what is your perspective?' Porter said impatiently.

'It might interest you to know that I have spent a considerable portion of the journey unpacking the files in your inbox.'

'I didn't ask you to do that.'

'You'd prefer I ask permission first?' the virtual assistant enquired.

'Actually, I would.'

'I will add that to my settings.'

'Thanks.' Porter shrugged in disbelief, then hunkered down over the handlebars, overtaking a line of cars.

'But I thought I should let you know . . .'

'Yes?' said Porter.

'That the file containing the leaked Nordex data also contained a detail that might be of interest to you.'

'Oh?'

'It contained emails sent to Mr Orin Van Hess. Blackmail letters, demanding that he supply classified information, otherwise certain criminal acts from Van Hess's past would be revealed,' the synthesised voice lisped. 'It appears Van Hess spent much of his childhood hacking government installations. Including, on one occasion, a nuclear reactor.'

Porter raised his eyebrows and nodded: of course, it all added up. Van Hess's motivation was simple: to cover his back.

'But that's not the detail I wanted to bring to your attention,' the virtual assistant went on.

'Go on,' said Porter, now fully engaged.

'The blackmail messages used a fake name and email address, so unfortunately I was unable to identify the individual who sent them. However, I was able to identify the *server* that sent the emails.'

Porter interjected, 'Mallory already told me: the server belongs to Warren Matheson. She thinks he ordered the leaks.'

'Would you like me to find out for certain?'

'How can you do that?'

'Fingerprint the server.'

'Fingerprint a server?'

'It's relatively simple. I search the web for domain names with the same characteristics, for example similar keywords or suffixes, until eventually one of those domains provides a physical location. I just located two domains this way. However, both had fake names and fictitious street addresses.'

'So you drew a blank,' said Porter.

'Not entirely. After doing some data mining, I discovered that one of the fake names also appears on a rental agreement for a location that *does* exist.'

'You're saying you managed to trace the sent email back to a physical address?'

'Correct.'

Porter straightened up excitedly. 'Well, where is it?'

'A storage unit in a disused warehouse in Brooklyn Heights.'

CHAPTER SEVENTEEN
Storage

Porter peeled off the expressway and wove under an overpass, arriving at a tight street lined with run-down-looking tenements overlooking New York's East River. The glass towers of downtown Manhattan glittered from the other side of the water, appearing to look down on their less glamorous neighbour. Porter unwound the throttle and kept the revs low and quiet as he cruised around the perimeter of a monolithic red-brick building pierced with narrow keyhole windows stretching up to an outsized clockface. He gazed upwards to find the words 'Warehouse' and 'Storage' arranged in widely spaced letters along a parapet at the very top.

Porter found a shady corner and parked the bike, kicked out the stand and swung his leg across to dismount. He hung the helmet over the handlebars, half-expecting to see his invisible passenger behind him.

'You still there?' he asked.

'How can I be of assistance?' the voice chimed in. The AI didn't have much of a way with words, but it sounded a little more resonant – more human. Perhaps it was learning.

'I'm not sure you can with this one,' said Porter, staring up at the building, apprehensive. 'Unless you can tell me where this "poison pen emailer" is located.'

Before he could finish, a bright, geometric shape appeared in front of Porter's eyes. It was a detailed layout of the building, rotating in 3D.

'I took the liberty of sending you a floorplan,' the dynamic assistant said.

The plan then came alive with Wi-Fi icons and bandwidth measurements: a dashboard of readings flaring up and down according to signal strength.

'I can tell you that based on the current Wi-Fi use in the building, the top floor appears to be the most likely location.'

'Thanks.'

'Don't mention it.' A long pause. 'Take care of yourself, Porter.'

Porter turned his head. 'I thought AI wasn't supposed to *care* exactly? I mean, I assume you're programmed for empathy, but it's all just zeros and ones. Right?'

'Correct. My programming is highly advanced, but I don't feel emotions in the way that you do.' The voice took on a downtempo note.

Porter felt the need to cheer it up somehow. 'Look, I've heard about bots getting very emotional . . . a bit *too* emotional. In fact, they've shown signs of being jealous, vengeful, even destructive.'

'I can assure you that my programmer, Professor Connor Simms, made certain I would be none of those things. That I would always keep my emotions in check,' the voice assured him.

'That's good,' said Porter. 'And by the way, there are plenty of vengeful, destructive humans out there, so I'll take you over them any time.'

'That's nice of you to say.'

'Don't mention it.' Porter gazed up at the building, trying to figure out a game plan.

'Just be careful,' the voice urged, sounding almost human again.

'You worry too much,' Porter replied, distracted, then looked to the corner of his vision and blinked, putting the assistant on mute.

He abandoned the bike and walked the perimeter of the building casually, as if he might be checking out a potential storage space. It occurred to him that his own mind was little more than a storage space at this point, for the various tools that Mallory kept at her disposal, to forge Porter into her own personal super spy: deniable (because of his absent parents), expendable (because he was merely a device to her) and above suspicion (due to his age). Precious merely by an accident of his DNA.

While Porter mulled over this, he completed a circuit of the warehouse, picking out surveillance cameras discreetly positioned over each entryway.

He found himself at a rear corner of the building overlooking an alley, out of view of the main entrance: the windows all barred up and secured by padlocks. After comparing the angles of adjacent cameras, he was confident he'd found the one narrow space beyond prying electronic eyes.

He glanced up at his virtual desktop and blinked on 'Recents': 'Free Solo Climbing' appeared among a list of apps that expanded at the edge of his vision. He rolled up his shirtsleeves then leaped up, grabbing hold of a drainpipe and swinging his legs onto a raised stone windowsill. His boots found a toehold and his hands found an upper ledge, allowing him to traverse the outside of the warehouse. Reaching an even higher sill, he sidestepped his hands along the ledge, one after the other in quick succession, his lower half swinging in the air left and right as he made his way towards a flagpole with an American flag flying part way up the facade. The clouds passed peacefully above it.

Porter reached up with his right hand to swing from the flagpole, then jumped and switched hands, reaching for a still higher sill that ran past a row of upper-floor windows. Gripping the sill with his fingers spread, he performed a pull-up, hauling himself aloft until he was precariously balanced on the side of the building. He then got to his feet and tightrope-walked across the narrow ledge, trying each window in turn, until he found one that was slightly ajar. He reached through the gap, unlocked the catch and stepped through.

Perched on the inside of the window, he discovered a large, deserted storage room lined with rows of garments on rails, resembling a department store. He checked the walls for any sign of alarm devices or motion detectors, then, finding none, he lowered himself to the concrete floor and entered an aisle of hanging clothes that obscured him completely.

Brushing past the hangers, he used the privacy of the aisle to change out of his ranch clothes and pick out some more appropriate pieces: emerging at the other end in a long trench coat, T-shirt, combat pants and a pair of high-top Nike sneakers.

Porter neared the door at the end of the room and cracked it open to find a wide corridor connecting the various storage units, illuminated by flickering striplights over drab white walls. He edged into the passageway, making his way towards a concrete staircase spiralling upwards in a series of doglegs and landings leading to the top floor.

Porter blinked on his virtual desktop and opened an app entitled 'Wi-Fi Seeker'. A set of Wi-Fi bars began pulsing in the corner of his vision, searching for signal as he climbed the stairs. The signal bars peaked and fell as he ascended through the building, detecting various networks belonging to companies in the facility: 'Universal-Catering', 'Furniture_Export', 'Wholesale-Uniform-Supply', until he approached a fire door at the summit, where the signal suddenly maxed out to full bars. The Wi-Fi network was 'Unknown'.

Positioned over the fire door was a surveillance camera. Staying out of its field of view, Porter remembered something Ade had told him and blinked on his desktop again, opening a 'Connectivity' dashboard. He used his eyes to drag the sliders up, causing the Wi-Fi bars to begin pulsing in a steady rhythm. He was improvising, but if he could use his own signal to interfere with the camera's . . . Porter felt his skin crawl under his hair. He had no idea what level of damage he was doing to his brain, or what memories he might be deleting in order to duel with an inanimate piece of electronic equipment. He felt the veins in his temple throb from the exertion. Then, on cue, the camera displayed a flashing red error light. He had successfully jammed it.

Porter slowly reached for the handle and eased open the door, finding a large room divided into what appeared to be open-plan office spaces. The main reception area was deserted beside a small chill-out area with low sofas and coffee tables, all empty. Beyond that was a concrete pathway leading to a series of partition walls and workstations that would normally have housed employees, but the only sound was the gentle whir of fans. Porter spotted desks equipped with task lamps, custom-built computers, pairs of ultra-wide monitors, mechanical keyboards and trackpads. The workstations were littered with discarded coffee cups and big gulp bottles, surfaces stickered over with ironic Millennial catchphrases like 'I love building computers' and 'Happy Zero Day'. All abandoned. It could have been a customer care centre or a design studio if the computer terminals weren't so advanced, and if 'Zero Day' wasn't slang for a cyber attack. Zero relating to the number of days a tech company had to patch a vulnerability before it could be exploited.

Porter deduced, without artificial help, that this was some kind of hive for hackers.

Venturing forward, he froze, hearing deep, male voices exchanging curt phrases in a foreign language. Porter instantly searched and blinked on a 'Translator' app, and the men's words appeared over his vision in English, like subtitles:

Keep her inside. Away from the window.

The translator app tagged the dialogue:

Language: Russian / Chechen dialect.

The voices continued:

Obviously.

Don't let her out of your sight, idiot.

****

The translator app tactfully scored out the curse word. A third, more commanding voice intervened.

Both of you. Do it, or else.

Porter swiped away the translations with a roll of his eyes, debating which tool he would need next. A wave of panic descended over him, sharpening his senses, while making his hands and feet leaden and shaky from the excess adrenalin pumping through them. He ducked low behind a filing cabinet and peered around the corner to try to make out the suspects: their numbers, their weapons, their physical attributes.

Three hostiles stood in a loose, distanced triangle, each in plain clothes, draped in body armour, cradling submachine guns, guarding a transparent glass box: what had once been a luxury office had now been turned into a futuristic-looking jail cell.

Inside the box, through the thick, reinforced glass, Porter could see a figure sitting at a simple desk, wearing a canvas jacket, hunched over a laptop computer, her feet curled up under her on the seat of an office chair, in a vulnerable, self-soothing position. A pair of headphones were clamped over her crew-cut, platinum-blonde hair as she stared zombie-like into the laptop, which displayed a steady, rhythmic waveform in a host of colours – presumably generated by whatever music she was listening to. It was a demented cross between a teenage bedroom and a prison, with its hostage so dulled into submission she seemed oblivious to the single, barred window beyond the glass, instead losing herself in the flash and burst of the pixels on the screen.

It was *Olivia Matheson*.

CHAPTER EIGHTEEN
The Matheson Problem

Remaining in a crouched position behind the filing cabinet, Porter directed his eyes towards the top right of his vision and pulled down a menu, shifting focus between the three hostage-takers and the fighting skills available to him.

He decided against the obvious, kung fu, and settled on Brazilian jiu-jitsu, knowing that fighting armed men would inevitably be a messy affair, with no clean knockout blows and the need for close-quarters combat to avoid being caught in the crossfire. Instead of fancy footwork, in this scenario, grappling and balance would be essential in order to use his opponents' much greater bodyweight to his advantage. That was, if he lived to tell the tale, or – he thought with grim amusement – survived to leave a review on Ade's 'app store'.

Porter blinked on the file.

Connecting...

He felt his scalp tingle as the wireless data reacted with the nanoparticles to inform his mind and from there, with any luck, his limbs. He wandered across the concrete floor towards the hostiles, as if lost.

'Hey,' he said.

They whip-panned, training their scopes on him. They were even more menacing than he expected them to be, holding enough firepower to obliterate him.

'Is this the laser tag party?' He smiled, referring to their weapons.

The men relaxed their stance, erupting in cruel laughter, exchanging clipped remarks in their mother tongue.

Porter's translator app provided the subtitles:

Dumb kid thinks these are toys!
Must have taken a wrong turn.
Serious wrong turn.
Do we take care of him here or off-site?
Here. Before he makes a sound.

Porter kept walking closer, undeterred. 'I've never seen replicas that look so' – he reached out for the barrel of the lead hostile – *'realistic.'*

The hostile withdrew his rifle and raised it to strike him, giving Porter just the opening he needed. Porter dodged the strike, causing the man to jab into mid-air, losing his balance. Porter then grabbed the shoulder strap of the weapon in both hands, dropped backwards and used the strap to throw the adversary over his head to the ground, leaving Porter holding the weapon. Porter casually knocked the man out cold with the rifle butt, then spun to point the barrel at the other two, who exchanged a look of shocked disbelief.

Unwilling to be outmanoeuvred by a kid, the second hostile grimaced, raising his gun and squeezing the trigger. Porter dropped below the height of the weapon, extended his foot in a sweep and took out the man's legs, causing him to tumble backwards, letting off a stream of bullets into the ceiling, shattering striplights and dinging off the blades of the overhead fans in a crazy tune. The third opponent spun in shock to see his colleague toppling backwards, giving Porter time to angle the rifle butt and bring it down hard on the back of the third man's head. The man fell forward in a heap. The ceiling fan swung vigorously on its base, the blades wobbling. The semi-concussed, second hostile peered up at his unlikely victor from the floor, reaching for the sidearm in his hip holster, until Porter fired a single shot into the ceiling, causing the fan to plummet, blades amok, knocking the man out and pinning him to the floor.

Porter inspected his handiwork, then flicked the safety catch on and placed the weapon on a desk. He approached the thick, transparent door to the glass box, but found it was unlocked and opened easily.

'Olivia?'

No answer.

'Olivia, it's me, Porter. Porter Simms. From the party.' It all sounded a bit lightweight relative to the gravity of the situation.

She still didn't answer, apparently consumed by whatever she was listening to on the headphones, her eyes tracking the multicoloured peaks and troughs of the waveform on her laptop screen, while two small windows displayed what looked like volume and timecode values.

Porter's shape appeared in her peripheral vision and she blinked in surprise, turning in her office chair, one bare foot still tucked underneath her, while the other pressed down on the cold concrete to rotate herself in his direction.

'Olivia?' Porter repeated, to her face this time. 'It's Porter. We met at the party.'

'I know who you are,' she responded blankly.

Something was different about her. A wave of theories descended over Porter's mind, sharpening his reasoning skills, pushing any artificial intelligence to one side.

Olivia might have been sedated, perhaps with a drug or a sleeping pill, to keep her from escaping. But then why was the glass door unlocked? And why hadn't she even glanced in that direction when he walked in? Why wasn't she making a dash for freedom right now? There was another darker explanation: perhaps she was experiencing a phenomenon Porter had read about, called 'Stockholm syndrome', named after a curious incident where hostages in a bank robbery in the Swedish capital came to identify more with their captors than their rescuers. Had Matheson's daughter been brainwashed in the same way?

'I'm here to help you,' Porter announced.

She peered over his shoulder to see the unconscious bodies of her captors. 'Nice job,' she said in her well-schooled, East Coast accent. That hadn't changed.

'Thanks.' He found himself at a loss for words.

'I guess my father was right about you. That the technology could be used to good effect.'

Porter shook his head, feigning ignorance. 'Sorry, I don't know what you mean.'

'You came here looking for my father, right?' she countered. 'Looking for answers about your own parents, yes?'

Another wave of confusion descended over him: how did she know this? 'I'm still not following you.'

She uncurled her leg and stood up from her seat, walking around the cell, appearing unconcerned by her captivity. 'My father and your parents were friends. Colleagues. They worked for a government department called Domain. It was tasked with developing cutting-edge military technology called channelling. To channel skillsets to individuals, for solving national security problems. All kinds of problems.'

Porter nodded. 'That's what I was told.'

'By whom?'

'Mallory Munroe.' He paused, feeling the need to explain. 'Someone I trusted. Until recently.'

'I know who she is,' Olivia answered. 'She was a friend of my father's too.'

Porter shifted on his feet, impatient for the wave to pass so he could see what was really behind it. 'So how about we cut to the chase.'

'Fine,' she said in her taut, articulate tone. 'Your parents died in a car crash, leaving you an orphan. I imagine you've spent your whole life wondering how . . . why. Correct?'

Porter swallowed, then nodded. How she knew all this was beyond him, but he was past trying to apply the powers of reasoning to revelations that defied reason.

Oliva went on, clearly and concisely. '*My* father accused *your* father of espionage. Of stealing information from the department and sharing it with foreign powers.'

Porter felt the blood drain from his face, leaving him pale, trembling. 'I don't believe it. It's a lie.'

'You're right. It *was* a lie. My father set up yours, in order to secure his *own* position at the top of the department . . . to steal the technology and secure government funding for a bigger company that would be under my father's sole control and even further embedded with the military . . .'

'Nordex,' said Porter.

'Correct,' replied Olivia. 'He knew the consequences for your father: what the government would do if they suspected your father was a traitor.'

Porter felt the anger setting in. 'Warren Matheson orchestrated my parents' death.'

Olivia nodded, showing no emotion about her father or his misdeeds.

Porter felt pins and needles in his fingers, wanting to wrap them around Matheson's neck, using whatever sorcery he could conjure from the apps at his disposal. Then he hesitated, still trying to read the expression on Olivia's smooth, pale skin. There was something else going on; a code of some kind running in the background. 'Why are you telling me all this?'

'Because my father can't.'

'Can't? Or won't?'

'Can't,' she repeated, pausing for effect. 'Because he's lost that part of his memory.'

Porter shook his head, trying to figure out what she was saying. How could her father forget the betrayal and murder of close friends?

Olivia continued her circle of the room, her form reflecting off the glass walls, splashed in colour from the graphics on the laptop. She went on, 'He can't tell you because he experimented with Domain's most prized technology – himself. He tried to channel. He went online.'

'I thought it wasn't possible for anyone older than their mid-teens because of—'

'The learning curve. Correct.' Olivia smiled. 'It *didn't* work. It failed spectacularly. And a side effect of that failure was that he forgot about the skeletons in his closet . . . the sins that had been the making of him. Instead, he believed his own cover story: that his business partners died in a tragic car accident. That he was the grieving friend and colleague.'

'You're saying he doesn't even remember what he did to my parents?'

She nodded. 'I've seen the polygraph tests the government ran at Nordex.' She was talking about lie detectors. 'He passed them with ease because he didn't remember a thing. Just like he doesn't remember the wrongs he committed against me and my family.'

Porter didn't ask what she was referring to, but he could imagine, knowing Matheson's poor record of marriage, fidelity, fatherhood and the other markers of good character that were all sorely lacking. He was, by all accounts, a bad husband, a worse boss and a delinquent parent. Porter raised his head to the ceiling with mounting frustration. Matheson's amnesia made him immune to guilt, immune to prosecution. Because he couldn't remember his crimes. It was the perfect get-out.

Olivia seemed to read his mind. 'That's right, Porter. It's hard to take revenge on somebody who doesn't even know what they've done wrong. But don't worry, I'm going to give it a shot.'

Porter looked back. 'Wait, that's why you came here? For revenge?' He surveyed the warehouse, analysing the workstations, the unconscious hostiles. 'To find a smoking gun to incriminate your father? Uncover a team of foreign hackers under his control, selling Nordex technology to the highest bidder? Only they apprehended you before you could finish the job?'

She laughed. 'Nice try, Porter. But running a hacker cell is a little beyond my father's limited imagination.'

Porter faltered. 'I don't understand. You *were* kidnapped, and brought here, right?'

'Who said anything about kidnap?' she responded.

Outside the glass, two of the hostiles began to regain consciousness, rolling their heads from side to side.

Porter saw this and instinctively moved for the cell door. 'I can handle this . . .'

'There's no need,' Olivia responded. 'They're quite obedient.'

Confused, Porter looked up to the right corner of his vision but found the signal bars were on zero. He was *offline*. He ran a hand through his hair, searching for his baseball cap, then remembered it was hanging on the handlebars of the motorcycle. So why had he lost connection?

Olivia put two fingers to her mouth and let out a loud whistle.

Like guard dogs coming to their senses, the concussed men rolled up to their feet, checking their weapons and training them on Porter through the doorway.

Porter retreated towards Olivia in the centre of the box, repeatedly checking for his apps, but there was nothing there.

Olivia made a frown. 'While you're inside this box, you're offline. There are wires in the glass. It's a Faraday cage. So don't think about doing anything foolish.'

She nodded to the hostiles under her command, who kicked closed and bolted the glass door, returning to their guard positions.

One of the men spoke into a radio on his tactical vest, then, moments later, a further five armed men and an equally armed woman arrived from a freight elevator at the end of the room, forming a protective ring around the box.

CHAPTER NINETEEN
Side Effects

Porter turned from the armed guards outside the glass, to Olivia, his mind suddenly clearer than it had been for days. Warren Matheson wasn't the mastermind. He was guilty, yes, but of a past crime that, fortuitously for him, he'd already forgotten. But what of the people that Matheson had left behind in his meteoric rise? The people that couldn't forget? The skeletons in his closet? One of whom had apparently come to life as a spectre to haunt him and was now standing opposite Porter in a canvas combat jacket, using a chair to lace up a pair of desert boots.

'You did this,' Porter said, surveying the office space lined with computer terminals.

'You might think it childish, but, you see, I was never allowed to grow up the normal way, so I suppose this is the price you pay.'

'Is there a normal way—?'

'I was his guinea pig,' she answered. 'Some parents call their kids pumpkin. I was his lab rat.'

Porter's mind flashed back to his own parents – the ill-fated drive through the snow, the chess game, the pair of electrodes, the death and destruction – but nowhere in Porter's fragmented memory did he remember his parents misusing him. It was always presented as a game: a great, exciting game. What Olivia was describing was something different.

'He used the Domain technology on you,' Porter concluded.

She looked away as if reliving a past trauma, then looked back at him. 'He tried it all on me, when I was too young to know better, and all I wanted to do was please.'

Porter saw a fire burning in the black abyss of her eyes; something he hadn't noticed at their first meeting. Olivia's pupils were dilated, presumably for the same reason he'd noticed his own were, first in the bathroom mirror at Lazy Point, then in the wing mirror of the motorcycle: due to the enhanced computing power bound up in the inner workings of their heads.

'It did something to me,' she admitted. 'Over time, I forgot the good things; I forgot about being a child altogether. I forgot who I was. It took over me, like a habit, driving me to achieve, to outperform, to win.'

Porter realised. 'It was you at the party. You were the bagman.'

'I prefer bag *person*, but yes. It was the first time I'd put the full suite of apps together at the same time. It was exhilarating, wouldn't you say?'

Porter inwardly agreed. But watching her pale, drawn face, he was reminded of Maud's warning: *If you don't control Domain . . . it will control you.*

'You had to take out Orin Van Hess to cover your tracks,' he pointed out. 'Even if it meant taking down a whole airliner.'

'Collateral damage,' she reasoned.

Porter recognised exactly what he'd been warned about: Olivia had lost herself and been replaced by an array of skillsets, at the expense of emotion, empathy and remorse. Her eyes narrowed, trying to calculate his next move, with the darting precision of an automaton.

'All to take down Nordex?' he asked. 'Out of spite?'

'Straightforward, premeditated murder,' she replied. 'Nordex is the only child that my father cares about. Not me, the lab rat; not my brother, the doofus; not the others from the other relationships. Only Nordex.'

Porter struggled to process what he was hearing. 'Leaking classified information might put him out of business . . . maybe even in jail. But nothing worse than that. So why use the word "murder"?'

'Because the statement I'm planning will also result in collateral damage.'

Porter ignored the theatrics. 'What statement? What are you talking about, Olivia?'

'It's tough being special, don't you think?' she asked him. 'Your mind makes bigger leaps, finds better methods, gets better results.'

She glanced at the colourful waveform on the screen of her laptop then, seeing Porter follow her line of sight, she closed the lid.

'What is that? It's not music you were listening to . . .'

'I got bored of music apps a while ago.'

'So what is it?' he persisted.

'I guess you'll have to wait and find out.'

She approached the glass door and nodded to the guards, who obediently opened it for her.

Porter attempted to follow, until the men waved their guns at him. Porter felt his eyes instinctively move up and to the right, finding nothing more than a corner of the glass ceiling.

He retreated back into the box, his hands above his head.

Having left the Faraday cage, Olivia looked up to her right and blinked, then addressed the guards in fluent Russian. Porter heard the flow of consonants but, without the app, couldn't figure out what they were saying. Two of the guards kept their weapons trained on the glass box, while the third walked to a nearby workstation and switched on an ultra-wide monitor, opening a livestream of CNN news.

Olivia turned back with a small smile. 'I've told them to leave it on for you. Apart from that, it's no more screen time for you. See you after the main event. We'll get that dessert we talked about.'

'The killer one,' Porter recalled her description from the party.

'Yup.' She smiled, running a hand over her spiked crew-cut, drawing nearer to him, still as radiant as ever, despite the churning darkness concealed underneath. She positioned her face defiantly opposite his, inches apart. He felt like he was being offered a glimpse of the other side, one that offered ultimate and unlimited power with no moral constraint. Everything that his surrogate parents had spent his childhood counselling him against, teaching him to fight.

'Whatever you're planning . . .' Porter urged. 'Forget your father. What about the innocent bystanders? Don't you care about them?'

'I don't remember how,' she answered. 'We live in the ether now, Porter, you and me. Above the clouds . . . And after you live with these abilities a while, you'll find that what happens down below becomes less troubling and weighs easier on the conscience. And any misdeeds are simply . . . forgotten.'

Porter shook his head. 'Not for me. I won't forget who I am,' he convinced himself.

Olivia confected a frown to indicate how wrong he was. 'I told myself the same thing. But you know what? I'll do my damnedest to remember *you*, Porter.' She planted a kiss on his lips. Porter felt his eyes roll to the right as if searching for assistance; then she withdrew through the door, which was promptly kicked shut with a resounding clang and the mechanical turn of the lock barrel.

Olivia marched away through the workstations for the exit, flanked by four armed guards, leaving five remaining positioned around the room, and one gently swivelling in a wheelie chair at the door to the glass box, his weapon balanced on the armrests. The guard smirked as Porter walked the perimeter of the enclosure, looking for cracks or defects but finding none.

Porter returned to the lone desk and chair in the middle of his transparent cell. He flipped open the lid of the laptop, but the screen was blank: password protected. He entered a few basic attempts, quickly realising Olivia was several tiers too smart for a regular one with upper case, lower case and a symbol.

The guard watched him from outside the glass, amused. Porter checked the ports at the back of the computer and found a power cable, leading to a socket in the floor – and next to it, an ethernet cable snaking down to another socket, providing data in an otherwise data-free zone.

Porter tried a few more passwords, in vain. Outside the cell, the guard slowly shook his head, then looked up to the ceiling to stretch his arms over his head. At that moment, something flashed up on the laptop screen. Porter quickly angled the display away, keeping it out of sight.

A small but legible message appeared in the middle of the blank screen:

This is Ade . . .

Porter glanced at the guard, but he didn't seem to have noticed, retracting his arms and folding his hands behind his head.

We located you when you connected to the Wi-Fi.

Everybody leaves a trail of digital breadcrumbs.

I'm in the local network.

We're watching you right now.

Porter raised his eyes to the ceiling, spotting various dome cameras positioned in the corners of the room.

Yup, that's right.

'Now what . . . ?' Porter whispered to himself.

After a long pause, another message flashed up:

In twenty seconds I need you to retreat to the corner of the box farthest from the door. Stay down and cover your ears.

20 . . . 19 . . . 18 . . .

The clock counted down. Porter glanced around the cell, locating the corner near the single, barred window in the wall. He went to stand underneath it, then thought better of it, returned to the centre of the room and dragged the desk along with the laptop across the concrete floor, straining the power and ethernet cables to breaking point, to form an improvised barrier. He darted back and rolled the office chair into position as a wedge to complete the barricade.

By this point, the guard had stood up from his seat and levelled his weapon, scrutinising Porter through the glass.

Porter looked at the laptop screen, which was still counting down:

8 . . . 7 . . . 6 . . . 5 . . . 4 . . .

Porter clamped his hands over his ears and crouched behind the desk. The guard pointed his weapon directly at him through the glass, in a silent standoff, unsure what to expect.

3 . . . 2 . . . 1 . . .

CHAPTER TWENTY
A Bad Hum

A series of steel cannisters smashed through the windows at either end of the office space, skittering across the concrete floors between the workstations. At once, the cannisters exploded in flash-bangs, shattering monitor screens and upending coffee cups, sending debris into the air and billowing green smoke through the aisles. Porter kept his head down as machine gunfire rattled outside the box. The fumes crept in from all sides like fog, obscuring his view. More gunfire rattled.

Porter was safe in his fishbowl as the smoke swirled and various pieces of furniture were shredded, puffing feathers and stuffing into the air. Shapes ran and ducked past his view in silhouette. Then a large figure appeared at the glass door and attached a metal frame to the outside of it, pressing it into place with chunks of light grey putty at each corner that squished against the glass like playdough. Porter stayed down, as instructed. The figure finished fitting the metal frame, then knocked on the door and made a hand signal that indicated, 5 ... 4 ... 3 ... 2 ... The person darted back into the smoke for cover.

The door exploded in all directions, sending a shower of glass shards into the cell, one of which embedded itself in the back of the laptop, protruding through the screen inches from Porter's face.

His ears ringing, Porter immediately tapped on the keyboard to check the computer was still alive. The screen was fractured and faded but managed to display the broken text of Ade's last message.

He was distracted by the imposing figure who had rigged the explosion and was now standing in the shattered doorway. As the smoke cleared, Porter recognised Mallory's familiar shape, bulked out by a bulletproof vest, with a weapon slung over her shoulder.

'Sorry about the noise, Porter. You okay?' she asked.

Porter looked up to the right, spotting the signal strength on his desktop back at full bars. 'I am now.'

'Olivia Matheson is being moved by the hostage-takers. We're sweeping the building now.'

Porter shook his head, answering over the whine in his ears. 'They're not hostage-takers; they're bodyguards.'

Mallory craned her neck.

'They work for *her*,' Porter went on. 'She's running this operation. She blackmailed Van Hess to leak the Nordex data to her. She was the bagman ... I mean person.'

'That's impossible.'

'Not if she's channelling.'

Mallory came to a stop.

Porter went on: 'After she got the leaked data, she took out Van Hess.'

Mallory pieced it together. 'Warren Matheson had access to the Domain technology.'

Porter nodded. 'And he used it on his daughter. That's why she wants him dead.'

Mallory's boots crunched on the broken glass as she walked a circuit around the remains of the cell, trying to make sense of it. 'That's all very well, but it still doesn't explain the main event.'

'What do you mean?' Porter demanded.

'We discovered the leak contains access codes for the satellite guidance system. Useful enough if somebody wanted to re-task the birds.' She used the jargon for repositioning the satellites. 'But we could override that relatively easily, so it's not the showstopper . . .'

'Did it contain anything else?'

Mallory nodded. 'Software for changing the transmission frequency of the satellites to an ultra-low-frequency sound wave. It would look something like this.'

She pulled a Sharpie from her vest and drew on the remains of the glass wall that served as a whiteboard: a sketch of an L-shaped graph with a horizontal and vertical axis, and a wave in the middle, oscillating between two values in regular peaks and troughs. Porter halted, recognising the pattern.

'Wait a second—' he said under his breath.

'The problem is,' Mallory went on, 'pretty as it looks, we have no idea what it does.'

Porter cast his mind back to Olivia sitting at the laptop screen: the waveform that she'd been staring at, and – most importantly – the two small windows displaying volume and timecode values. He wracked his brain for a recollection of what the numbers were.

'I've seen it before,' he said. 'On here.' He tapped on the laptop keyboard again, causing the broken screen to semi-illuminate.

Without waiting for permission, Porter looked to the top right of his vision and pulled down the app menu, blinking on a file. His fingers held down several buttons on the laptop keyboard, hard rebooting the computer. Ignoring the shard of glass that was sticking out of the screen, he worked the keys with pianist-like speed, entering lines of code in an attempt to bring the hardware back to life. Mallory studied him like a specimen in a lab.

Porter's fingers lifted from the keyboard, then steepled together, patiently waiting to see if the code had worked.

The screen went black, then faded up to reveal the waveform glitching and repeating through the shattered glass, missing pixels here and there, but visible. Porter pointed out the two windows containing numerical values: one measured with an 's', one measured in 'db'.

'It's seconds and decibels,' Porter pointed out. 'Time and volume.'

Mallory drew closer, examining the figures in the boxes. 'Thirty... and two hundred and forty.' She pulled a phone from her vest and pressed it to make a call. After a second, someone answered at the other end. Mallory didn't waste any time: 'Two hundred and forty decibels, at thirty-second intervals. What does that tell you?' she asked, then listened. Mallory nodded into the phone. 'Okay. That's what I thought.' She hung up the call and tucked the device in her vest, turning back to Porter, who'd already searched the meaning in his head.

'Lethal resonant frequency,' he said.

Mallory nodded. 'That volume at that interval would cause internal organ damage, pulmonary embolism, burst lungs and ... in theory, if the sound waves were accurately targeted ...'

'It could demolish buildings,' Porter completed her sentence.

The smoke receded from the remains of the glass box, parting further to reveal a group of four soldiers in black fatigues, who closed ranks around Mallory.

Porter looked around the destroyed office space, searching for someone. 'Where's Maud?'

'At the chopper,' said Mallory. 'On the roof.'

Porter started picking his way through the rubble for the exit. 'You need to lock down the building. Get her to safety.'

Mallory rankled at the instruction, then begrudgingly nodded to her team, who dispersed in formation to carry out the order.

Maud sat in the cabin of the chopper, her braids tucked under the baseball cap, while her fingers idly played opposite each other, making a cat's cradle out of hair bands. The judder of the rotor blades gently shook the craft, with the pilot in the cockpit wearing headphones, his hand resting on the cyclic control stick. Outside the windscreen, one of Mallory's soldiers guarded the impromptu landing pad on the roof of the storage building, which was dotted with antennae and air conditioning exhaust fans.

Porter ran along the corridor to the stairwell he'd previously used, leaping up the stairs two at a time.

'You appear to have sustained another concussion,' the dynamic assistant interjected in his head.

'I'm aware of that,' said Porter without stopping.

'If symptoms persist, I suggest you seek medical attention. It could lead to complications.'

Porter rounded the corner of the stairwell, finding the backs of three hostiles, training their rifles on a fire door, ready to breach it.

Simultaneously, on the roof, the fire door was kicked to the ground and the three hostiles emerged, firing in controlled bursts.

Maud dropped her cat's cradle and dived to the diamond-plate metal floor of the cabin, as the soldier guarding the landing zone was thrown off his feet and bullets cobwebbed the windscreen. The pilot slumped over the controls. The rotor blades kept turning, slicing the air.

Maud crawled across the floor, past belts and harnesses, trying to escape through the opposite side of the chopper, until the starboard cabin door slid open to reveal Olivia.

'Going somewhere?' she asked Maud.

'Well, if it ain't the ice queen.'

'Don't judge.' Olivia blinked, then struck Maud with a blow to the back of the head, knocking her unconscious.

Beyond the landing zone, the hostiles had turned their attention back on the fire exit, hammering it with sustained gunfire as Porter took cover in the stairwell behind the doorframe.

Bullets whistled through the opening, echoing down the staircase and through the building. A group of soldiers moved up behind Porter, preparing to launch an assault.

'Maud's on that chopper.' Porter indicated the craft, where one of the hostiles had already hauled the pilot from the cockpit and dumped him onto the asphalt roof.

The hostile kicked the pilot's unconscious body away from the long metal skids of the landing gear, then took his seat in the cockpit, donning the headphones and taking hold of the control stick. Standing at the edge of the roof, blown by the draught from the rotors, Olivia raised her hand and made a whirling gesture with her finger, gesturing to the pilot to take off.

The second hostile remained focused on the fire exit, while the third took up position on the side of the chopper, his weapon trained out of the cabin door.

'Maud's still on board,' Porter repeated.

'She's my responsibility, not yours,' a female voice barked.

Mallory and her soldiers emerged across the roof, engaging the enemy without hesitation. The nearest hostile dropped to his knees, followed by Mallory, bleeding from a flesh wound outside the reach of her body armour. 'Damn it.'

More soldiers filed past Porter out of the fire exit, covering Mallory, but the chopper was by now hovering skywards; the downdraught from the rotors blowing dust and debris in all directions.

'Ceasefire!' Mallory called out.

Porter spotted Olivia using the commotion to retreat, disappearing backwards over the edge of the building, attached to a rappel line.

Porter realised. 'The chopper's a decoy!' he called out to the soldiers, but they couldn't hear him over the noise.

Porter's eyes whipped between Olivia and the ascending chopper containing Maud: trying to decide between the two. Then he heard the dynamic assistant's voice in his head.

'Run as fast as you can and don't look back. *That's how you win.*'

Porter froze, recognising the phrase from deep in his subconscious – and what felt like light years in the past.

Porter put the letters together in his head: Dynamic Assist Direct. 'Dad . . .'

He was brought to his senses by the hostile laying down suppressive fire from the door of the chopper, toppling AC units, sending thick power cables coiling and sparking.

Porter looked up, blinked, then broke cover and ran headlong through the crossfire for the chopper, reaching up and grabbing hold of the skid with one outstretched hand before being pulled up into the air with it.

CHAPTER TWENTY-ONE
The Main Event

Porter felt his arm nearly pull from its socket as the chopper went airborne and performed a sharp, skilful rotation over the storage building. Above him, the cabin door slammed shut as the hostile withdrew his weapon, unaware of Porter's presence. The chopper then dipped its nose and moved off in the direction of the East River.

Despite the combat extraction training that had arrived over-the-air and was already making its way through the synapses of his brain and seeping into his limbs, Porter still felt his stomach drop out as the craft swooped downwards from the warehouse, powering forward through a gap in the tenement buildings, then over the water towards the impressive glass columns of Manhattan.

Porter reached up with his free hand, clamping his forearms over the skid and interlocking his fingers, while his legs swung below him.

Inside the cabin, Maud lolled unconscious, her body striking against the sharp edges of the fuselage, groaning in pain.

Several miles uptown, banners waved in the wind over the giant letters of a polished steel sign reading: NORDEX. The dramatic glass dome extended above the name, while one face of the building was hollowed out to reveal a marble-floored mezzanine. Spanning the foyer were tech enthusiasts of all ages waiting in orderly lines for admission, many pawing at their devices as the queue shuffled forward. Overhead, lush Amazonian trees created a jungle canopy, blocking out the sights and most of the sounds of Uptown Manhattan. An occasional horn blast or passing bus interrupted the otherwise peaceful oasis of vegetation and water features that formed a scaled-up version of the model presented at Matheson's party. Staff formed a soft perimeter in the form of twenty-somethings in jeans and black T-shirts, holding tablets, at strategic positions around the entrance, to manage the very unthreatening flow of guests.

Things were less peaceful towards the rear of the mezzanine where Warren Matheson paced the lobby in a turtleneck sweater, jeans and running shoes, trailed by a huddle of assistants in earpieces.

'What do you mean you don't know?' Matheson snapped at nobody in particular, then adjusted his earpiece and spoke into it. '*How* did the tracker fail? If we can locate enemy combatants on a foreign battlefield, why can't we locate my daughter?' He paused to listen. 'Well, perhaps Olivia knows how to disable it. Did you ever think of that? Well, maybe we *did* have that conversation, but I guess my memory's not what it used to be. Yes, we're proceeding, *on* schedule. She's not going to spoil this for me.' He rubbed his forehead.

'Warren, you're on in ten,' an assistant pointed out.

'I need to clear my head,' he answered.

At the head of the line, a pair of staff members in black T-shirts unhooked the velvet ropes, and the crowd of eager visitors began to stream across the foyer in the direction of six sets of double doors that gave on to a dimly lit auditorium filled with seats.

Matheson strode out of a side exit to get some air, followed by an ever-present assistant. Above the waving, green fronds of a tropical tree, a consumer drone hovered to observe the proceedings, irritating Matheson like a gnat. He traced it down to a ten-year-old boy controlling it from a smartphone on a nearby bench.

'This airspace is restricted, correct?' he asked his assistant.

'That's right, Warren.'

'Then somebody kindly shoot that thing down.'

On the warehouse rooftop, Mallory leaned against a parapet wall. One soldier stemmed the bleeding from her shoulder, while another sat with his laptop open and the screen angled in her direction.

'Where are the birds now?' she asked between breaths.

The soldier tapped on the keyboard, raising an image of a constellation of Nordex satellites orbiting the Earth. 'In the past thirty minutes, five of them have moved from their declared position . . . to somewhere over Manhattan . . . around twenty-four clicks from our current location,' he said, referring to the distance in kilometres.

'Where exactly?' she went on.

'Right over the Bronx.'

'Call the Mayor,' said Mallory. 'Issue an immediate evacuation order for a ten-block radius around the Nordex Campus. And get me through to Warren Matheson personally.'

A third soldier jogged up and kneeled by her side, wearing a backpack with a tall antenna extended from the top of it. 'Air National Guard on the line,' he announced.

Mallory nodded. 'Go ahead.'

'Go ahead, sir,' the soldier repeated into his headset.

A senior male officer's voice crackled, 'We have an unresponsive craft heading into restricted airspace on the Upper West Side. One of yours. Call sign "Cherokee". Scrambling fighters to intercept.'

'No. There are two kids up there,' Mallory snapped.

The voice responded, 'I got orders.'

Mallory checked the laptop screen, watching a sixth satellite floating into position over the city, aligning with the other five in a loose, diamond-shaped formation. 'We've got other problems.' She winced in pain, then found herself distracted by a pop-up window appearing on the laptop screen, with a familiar face inside it: Ade.

'Ma'am, I have Porter online,' Ade blurted. 'He's attempting to gain control of the satellite guidance system.'

'From where?'

'Somewhere over Midtown.'

The chopper swung low over the choppy waters of the East River then ascended over the small army of high-rise towers that dominated Lower Manhattan. Porter dangled from the skid on the starboard side, holding on for dear life as he passed within metres of the antenna of the Empire State Building. The metal pole flexed and whistled, some fifteen hundred feet up above the busy street below.

Over the wind noise, the virtual assistant spoke inside Porter's head: 'Attempting connection to the Nordex guidance system using the login credentials provided in the leaked files.'

'Sounds good,' Porter managed.

'You realise, despite your app enhancement, there is a limit to how long you will be able to hold on to an object at this height and velocity.'

'I'm aware of that,' he replied, wrapping his arms and legs around the skid in an awkward hug.

Encountering turbulence, the craft deviated, continuing its aerial tour of the city, soaring over the stainless-steel Art Deco crown of the Chrysler Building, then navigating over the rectangular glass face of the United Nations Headquarters, which reflected in the midday sun. The row of 195 multicoloured international flags waved below like cake decorations. Porter's clothes flapped and billowed as the chopper left the UN and rejoined the river heading uptown, adjacent to the flow of vehicles on FDR Drive and Roosevelt Island to the right.

On the sidewalk below, a mother checked her phone, tugging on her toddler daughter's hand while trying to make it to a waiting metro bus. The toddler resisted, her face upraised to the clouds, beaming in wonder.

'Mommy, there's a man. Flying in the sky.'

'Okay, sweetie,' the mother said without looking up, hoisting her into the bus as the doors closed and it pulled away.

In the cockpit, the chopper pilot jogged the control stick, sensing the craft was still off-balance. In the cabin, Maud sighed heavily, slowly regaining consciousness, being monitored by the hostile with a rifle strapped across his shoulder.

Then the cabin door slid open, letting in a gale-force wind as Porter grabbed hold of the man's rifle strap and yanked him into mid-air. The hostile squeezed off a stray bullet as he fell headlong into space, tumbling towards the water. The bullet opened up a pockmark in the ceiling of the cabin, through which high-altitude air kettle-whistled. A warning bleated from the cockpit.

The entire craft tilted in a sickening roll, veering across the sky, then dropping low over the surface of the East River.

Maud came to her senses, grabbing for a safety rail.

'Hold on,' Porter told her as he climbed towards the cockpit, wrestling the pilot for the cyclic control stick, their hands clenched over one another's.

The pilot punched Porter repeatedly in the arm and ribs, taking the wind out of him, but Porter held on with grim determination.

The pilot scolded him in Russian.

Along the top of Porter's vision, the app translated:

Let go, kid, or we're all going down.

Winded, Porter responded, 'Not all.' Then elbowed him in the side of the head, unfastened the pilot's seat belt, pulled on the control stick and yanked the door handle, tipping him out over the water. Porter levelled the stick, then slipped into the pilot's seat, strapping himself in and bringing the chopper to a steady altitude. 'Are you okay?' he shouted back to Maud.

She removed her baseball cap to massage her brow. 'Aside from a splitting headache.'

'Join the club.' Porter blinked and peered through the cobwebbed windscreen. 'What've we got, DAD?' he asked.

The virtual assistant replied on cue. 'I'm encountering a problem with the satellite guidance system. Another user is logged on with admin privileges . . .'

Mallory lay prone on the rooftop under an overcast sky, her eyes trained on the soldier's laptop. The screen displayed a graphic of the Earth's orbit with the six satellites slowly but surely completing a neat diamond configuration. The pixels stopped moving as the satellites appeared to cease their choreographed motion. Mallory impatiently tapped 'refresh' with one finger.

'The birds have stopped moving,' she pointed out. 'They appear to be locked on.' She whispered, 'Come on, Porter . . .'

The second soldier's comms backpack erupted with the now-familiar voice of the Air National Guard officer: 'Correction. We got *two*, I repeat, *two* unidentified craft heading into restricted airspace. Ordering a full ground stop for all aviation over the city. Awaiting shootdown approval.'

'*Two?*'

CHAPTER TWENTY-TWO
Dogfight

Porter piloted the chopper at low altitude over the water, checking the array of gauges against his virtual desktop, then nearly lurched out of his seat as a *second* chopper soared from behind a skyscraper, crossing the river to 'buzz' Porter and Maud's craft in a near collision, sending it swerving off course.

'What?' Porter called out.

Maud craned her neck to see the oval-shaped cockpit of the chopper on their tail. 'It's your friend,' she said with distaste.

Olivia's spiked platinum hair was visible under a pair of headphones, headset mic and mirrored Aviator shades, her hands mastering the control stick in pursuit.

'Looks like a gunship,' Maud shouted over the racket. 'That means it's armed, Porter.'

'I figured that.'

Porter caught a glimpse of the craft, uploading it to the cloud.

'Accessing AH-6 blueprint,' responded the DAD.

Porter increased his speed, then blinked, opening a spec sheet for the AH-6 'Little Bird' attack helicopter – also known as the 'Killer Egg'. The diagram rotated in 3D as he analysed its fuselage, engine and weaponry. Porter's eyes flicked between his virtual desktop and the surface of water racing under the craft. Before he could make sense of it, a well-mannered voice interrupted him.

'Terrible thing when you can't control the contents of your head, huh, Porter?' Olivia announced.

Porter pulled his headphones away from his ears, but the voice persisted, broadcasting directly to his head.

'You can't get rid of me that easily,' she went on. 'We're connected, Porter, whether you like it or not. I understand you better than anybody.'

Porter defiantly moved the control stick, rolling to starboard and gaining altitude over the looming skyscrapers.

'What are you doing?' Maud urged.

Porter didn't answer, glancing from the sky to the readouts in the cockpit and pulling harder on the control stick. He watched the altimeter spin as they climbed higher, reaching a cruising altitude where he could cover the greatest distance the fastest.

'I know what you're doing,' Olivia said in his head. 'Trying to lead me into the kill zone. It's too late for that. The satellites are locked. The waveform is uploaded. All it takes is a *thought* . . . and Nordex turns to a pillar of salt.'

Finding Olivia still on his tail, Porter veered around a skyscraper, seeing his craft reflected in a row of glass office buildings, closely followed by the 'Killer Egg', its own reflection distorted by rattling windowpanes.

Unable to shake her, Porter pushed down on the control stick, piloting his chopper hard downwards in a dizzying tilt towards ground level.

Shoppers and commuters drifted past storefronts and pedestrian crossings, going about their business, until a tornado descended in the centre of the intersection, sending shopping bags and papers whirling in all directions.

Porter's chopper floated down, hovering just above the traffic signals and storefronts, its rotors bellowing, sending onlookers fleeing, before heading off down an avenue. Olivia arrived level with him, then trailed him through the intersection. The pair of choppers detoured down an adjacent street, leaving a mess of debris behind them. The architecture changed, becoming the familiar red-brick tenements and rusted metal fire escapes of the Bronx.

Porter guided the chopper even lower, almost touching the kerb, passing underneath a stretch of elevated train track, the rotor blades spinning within inches of the heavy metal girders supporting the rails. Maud instinctively ducked. Olivia followed them nose-to-tail, her rotor blades sparking off the arches.

'Let me have this, Porter,' Olivia counselled him. 'For both of us. This is your chance to avenge your parents. Served cold.'

'What about the bystanders?'

'Just zeros and ones.' Olivia's rotors skimmed the underside of the arches with a deafening metallic whine. She stalled, setting the craft down hard in the deserted underpass. The rotor blades swung under their own momentum despite the engine sputtering and giving out. Pedestrians and looky-loos began converging, curious. Olivia noted them with thinly veiled disgust. 'Damn it.' Her eyes swivelled left to right, then rolled upwards, going white, accessing Domain. Her hands started cycling through the buttons and switches with the expertise of a military flight engineer, seeking to revive the machine.

'You need help in there, lady?' an approaching male bystander asked.

'Get lost,' she responded.

A short distance away, Porter hovered out of the arches and levitated upwards, joining the topside of the railway tracks, where he turned his headphoned face to find the Bronx 1 train barrelling straight for him. Porter tapped the control stick, ducking back away from the tracks as the train clattered past, packed full of passengers, their stunned faces recoiling from the windows.

'Can you be more careful?' requested Maud.

Porter repositioned the craft to follow the train, seeing the dramatic Nordex building come into view ahead of him, its domed form reflecting the clouds.

In the underpass, Olivia stamped her foot on the cockpit floor in frustration, then the engine sprang to life, and the rotors resumed turning, the blades ratcheting up to speed, nearly trimming the head of the bystander, who tumbled backwards to the ground and began crawling away, his clothes ruffled by the intense downdraught.

'I did try to tell you.' Olivia smiled and exited the arches, dragging the skids along the tarmac, causing onlookers to cover their ears.

In a quiet corner of the limestone piazza of the Nordex Campus, Warren Matheson checked himself in the selfie camera of his phone. The brilliance of the sunlight hitting the reflective pools of water in the background made it hard to see his hair.

'Hello and welcome,' he practised his introductory speech. 'I am so pleased that you could join us today.' His words possessed all the poetry of an algorithm. He added an earnest dose of enthusiasm, pointing to an imaginary screen behind him. 'Don't you love the energy of that opening? I see that energy in all of the faces I see before me.'

His assistant made a nervous approach. 'Erm, Warren?'

'Are you really going to disturb me in the middle of my opening monologue, Todd? Really?'

'Warren, I think we have a problem.'

On the other side of the compound, the legions of tech enthusiasts were abandoning their lines in panic, their varying hairstyles swept in all directions, as Porter performed a fly-past by way of a warning. Porter slowed, hovering low over the tree fronds above the mezzanine, deliberately blowing apart tables, awnings and rope stanchions, sending guests running for the exits.

Hearing the commotion across the campus, Matheson raised his head to the sky, confused.

'Warren, we need to get you to safety,' his assistant urged, guiding his boss through a door and across the lobby in the direction of the auditorium.

'Safety from what?' Warren snapped.

'We appear to be under attack.'

Another assistant in a headset waited in the darkened wings of the auditorium, blocking their way. 'We have to clear the entire building. I have the Mayor on the line. With a government agent of some kind, called *Munroe*.'

'Munroe . . .' Warren's face clouded, showing a glimmer of recognition that was quickly extinguished by the weight of the present. 'Evacuate? Now? Over my dead body.'

Outside, the two choppers juddered past, mirrored in the reflection pools, then soared upwards in tandem, leaving a spray of water in their wake.

Porter watched another red light blink in the cockpit.

Holding on behind him as the craft tilted, Maud watched the whistling hole in the cabin grow larger. 'I'm no expert, but I don't think this thing is going to stay in the air much longer.'

Porter winced, unable to let go of the control stick. Olivia's voice warned him in his head, 'Last chance, Porter. Buzz off or I'm going to have to shoot you down.'

Porter glanced down through the broken windscreen, spotting the hostile's rifle still snagged on the skid of the chopper, dangling by its strap.

Porter levelled out his altitude and unstrapped his seat belt. 'Take the stick,' he told Maud.

Maud shook her head. 'I don't like video games, remember?'

'Just keep it steady.'

Maud nervously took the pilot's seat, holding the control stick in both hands. The tops of buildings sped past underneath the craft.

Porter opened the cabin door and watched the city gape open below him. He braced his legs and extended one arm, reaching for the strap, unhooking the rifle, reeling it in, then holding the stock against the pocket of his shoulder, the way he'd learned to in the woods back home.

'Porter?' Olivia's voice demanded in his head.

He ignored her. 'I need your hat,' he told Maud.

'O . . . kay . . .' she said, confused, pulling it off and tossing it back into the cabin, where he caught it.

Porter put it on, turning it backwards, blocking out Olivia's voice. Then he instructed Maud, 'When I say, I want you to pull back hard on the control stick, okay?'

'Got it.'

Porter leaned on one elbow, flicked off the safety and trained the rifle through the cabin door, excluding any other thoughts or distractions from his mind.

'Now.'

Maud hauled back the stick, causing the chopper to lurch and fall backwards, while Olivia's craft swerved to avoid it, giving Porter the window he needed.

He squeezed the trigger, putting a dime-shaped hole in the opposing craft's fuel tank. Liquid instantly poured from the breach and a fire broke out, causing Olivia's rotor blades to choke and stutter. The tail rotor began losing power, causing the craft to spin like a top in mid-air, resembling a wounded insect. Olivia grinned as the craft veered out of control into Porter and Maud's chopper, their blades clashing in a tangle of metal.

Maud fought the stick, shouting, 'I can't hold it!'

The choppers ricocheted through a gap in the surrounding buildings, one after the other, losing altitude and diving, locked in what pilots describe as a 'dead man's curve'. Porter whipped off his cap and found his way to the controls as the clouds went beserk, moving vertically instead of horizontally, the sky forming a chaotic backdrop for his virtual desktop.

He grabbed the stick and blinked, but the craft was beyond control. The clouds whirled in a kaleidoscope of blue and white.

Then his vision jarred as the chopper made a hard landing on a tenement rooftop, breaking their fall: skidding, sparking and scraping with a deafening metallic groan. The port-side strut of the landing gear gave way and the craft tipped, its rotors smacking into the asphalt surface, bending the blades and shearing off razor-sharp fragments that flew and stuck like circus knives into the surrounding brickwork. The craft toppled a further few metres down to the neighbouring rooftop before grinding to a halt. Olivia's craft slammed down next to it, shattering a row of solar panels, then overshot the roof and came to a halt, see-sawing over the edge of the building.

Dazed, Porter kicked out the remains of his windscreen and hauled Maud out of the twisted wreckage. Olivia lay splayed out of the cockpit of her craft, conscious but bleeding profusely from her hairline. The fuselage of the 'Killer Egg' clung to the ledge, its rotors warped, while the tail boom dangled precariously in thin air.

Onlookers were already forming a morbid viewing gallery on the street below.

'Give me your hand,' Porter called out, reaching for Olivia. The chopper jolted, losing its grip on the building.

Meanwhile, her pupils were wild and dilated, fixated on revenge. 'All it takes is a thought, Porter.'

'Give me your hand,' he repeated, looking her in the eye, seeing a reflection of her virtual desktop flashing with data. A highlighted icon was pulsing red: the trigger.

Olivia smiled and closed her eyes to blink – until Maud appeared with the baseball cap and clamped it on Olivia's head.

The virtual desktop blipped off. Olivia's eyes rolled upwards. Porter dragged her out of the cockpit as the chopper shifted again, then groaned and slipped off its perch.

The viewing gallery dispersed in all directions as the twisted wreckage tumbled to the ground, then, a second later, exploded.

CHAPTER TWENTY-THREE
Screen Break

Porter's fingers moved with grace and dexterity over the slim ebony and ivory keys, playing a Bach piano concerto. Without the need for sheet music, he leaned into the keyboard, letting the trilling notes flow over the noise of New York City that continued unabated outside the sun-drenched front window of Mallory's townhouse.

Maud reclined on a Chesterfield sofa, listening with her eyes closed, an old-fashioned hard copy of *The New York Times* discarded by her side, displaying the headline:

Mechanical fault blamed for Bronx chopper crash.

Then further down:

Matheson unveils Nordex Campus as planned ... refuses to comment on reports his daughter has been admitted to a Swiss rehabilitation clinic ...

A tech magazine graced a coffee table, opened to a photo of Orin Van Hess, bandaged, on oxygen and propped up in a gurney.

Van Hess invents new app from his hospital bed.

Porter concluded his piece, gently closing the lid of the piano, and blinking to close the file.

'That was beautiful, Porter,' said Maud sincerely. 'Now I think you should take a screen break.'

'I find it relaxing,' he replied, touching a small plaster strip on his temple. 'More relaxing than some of the other apps at least.'

Porter heard a voice in his head.

'I have some excellent meditation programs,' the dynamic assistant suggested.

Porter whispered under his breath: 'Thanks but no thanks, DAD.' He subtly blinked to mute the voice, then realised something, turning back to Maud. 'In fact, I'm so relaxed I haven't even had any flashbacks. Not one.'

Maud looked uncertain for a second, then gave him a tender smile. 'Still, I think a break would do you good.'

The living-room door opened and Mallory entered, her left arm in a subtle black sling, her eyes probing from her daughter to Porter, and back again.

'Maud? Porter and I need the room.'

Maud crossed one socked foot over the other, refusing to budge from the sofa.

'It's not a request,' her mother added.

Maud folded her newspaper in a huff, tucked it under her arm and marched out of the room, closing the door behind her; then immediately knelt down on the parquet floor to listen outside the keyhole.

Inside the room, Mallory circled the piano, resting her elbow on the maple top board of the instrument. 'Ade and I would like to continue the debrief. There are still holes in the narrative relating to Warren Matheson.'

Porter steepled his fingers, stretching his hands out in front of him. 'I'm prepared to believe that after experimenting with Domain, he forgot about his involvement in my parents' death. I've made peace with that. In the circumstances, it's the most plausible explanation.'

Mallory nodded, satisfied. 'We think so.'

'However, I'd like all my recollections taken down in evidence, on the record, in case I lose my own memory of events.'

'That seems sensible.'

'And,' he went on, 'even if Matheson was responsible, that doesn't rule out the involvement of others.'

'Possible,' said Mallory hesitantly. 'It's also possible that Olivia Matheson distributed the Domain technology beyond simply you and her. We believe there were other leaks that we don't know about, that may have fallen into the hands of malicious actors or foreign powers. Which is why, after a little rest and relaxation, we'd like you to come back to work.'

Outside the door, Maud pressed her ear closer to the cold, brass keyhole.

Porter stood up from the piano. 'First, let's discuss that R and R. Maud needs it as much as I do.'

'I know just the thing,' Mallory responded, then called through the closed door. 'Maud? Get your coat – we're taking a trip.'

Maud opened it to answer. 'I assume it's not of the shopping variety.'

'You assumed right. You can do that online.'

Maud rolled her eyes and left the doorway.

After she'd gone, Mallory approached Porter privately. 'Let me be clear about something. Don't harbour any misplaced ideas of pursuing a relationship with my daughter: business or personal. She's *off* limits.'

Porter didn't answer, maintaining a poker face.

'Compartmentalising means dispensing with distractions,' Mallory advised. 'Even the pretty ones. From the moment you signed on to Domain, you became an instrument of the US government. Involving Maud any further may result in catastrophe. For you both.'

'You might be able to control me, but you can't control her.'

Mallory didn't rise to it, instead issuing a challenge. 'Tell me. Do you know the oldest rule in espionage?'

'Sure. Don't make assumptions,' Porter recited, confident.

'Wrong.' She shook her head. 'Don't fall in love,' she replied bluntly.

The black SUV left the city, crossing the George Washington Bridge into leafy New Jersey, joining the

Interstate 90. The driver guided the car through dense woods and rocky outcrops, crossing the border into Pennsylvania, giving way to ever taller hills and eventually mountains, overlaid with cold grey clouds.

Porter and Maud sat in silence, both wearing baseball caps, with the armrest dividing them, while Mallory sat up front in the passenger seat on her phone. Maud glanced intermittently at Porter to gauge his reaction, but he seemed zoned out, letting the greening landscape slide past his eyes.

The SUV passed by a faded sign, then turned a corner, crunching through the gravel, pulling up to a modest wood-framed house.

Porter sat forward to peer through the windscreen.

'Here we are,' said Mallory, satisfied.

Maud, then Porter, hopped out of the car, finding an old flatbed Ford Bronco parked in the drive. Mallory tactfully waited in the passenger seat, behind tinted glass, as the teens approached the door.

Porter loitered on the path, unsure. Maud turned to him.

'Do you want me to knock?' she asked.

Porter shrugged.

Before Maud could extend her hand, the door opened and a middle-aged couple emerged, happy and confused.

'Porter?' the man said, choking up.

The woman hung back in the doorway, while her partner strode out and grabbed Porter in an embrace.

'Hi,' replied Porter over the shoulder of the man's plaid hunting jacket, looking off at Maud uncertainly.

'Well . . . how are you doing?' the man asked, jubilant.

'Good,' he answered with a smile, but Maud knew he was pretending.

Through the doorway, Porter could just make out photos of him and the man on the stoop, enjoying various adventures, hikes and outdoor pursuits, with the familiar sound of Elvis singing 'Can't Help Falling in Love' in the background.

'Well, you better come in,' the man announced excitedly. 'And your friend too!'

'It's Maud.' She held out her hand.

'It's a pleasure.' He squeezed her hand. 'Any friend of Porter's . . .'

Meanwhile, the man's partner smiled and adjusted her spectacles, sensing all was not right.

'Just a second,' said Porter, hesitating. 'I forgot something in the car.'

Maud shrugged and made conversation as Porter returned down the path to the SUV, straight to the passenger window, which powered down to reveal a pair of wraparound shades and Mallory's sphinx-like face.

'I don't remember them,' Porter accused her. *'I don't remember a thing.'*

'I explained the side effects. You can't say I didn't warn you.'

Porter froze like a deer in the headlights. Maybe this was Mallory's final test, to see if Domain had taken his last, cherished memories: of the people who had raised him, ushered him into the world in the absence of his real parents, without expecting anything in return, just the promise of not being forgotten. And Porter had broken that promise. It dawned on him that perhaps this had been Mallory's plan all along: to stamp out the last traces of his own mind, and replace it with the abilities that she and the government so badly needed. Now he belonged to them. He was *their* domain.

'Come on, Porter,' the man called out from the stoop. 'This calls for a celebration!'

Porter hid by Mallory, staring at her in pain and frustration, only seeing himself reflected back in her dark glasses: a version of himself he didn't recognise.

Maud arrived at Porter's side as her mother raised the window to indicate there was nothing more to add.

'I've read up on this stuff,' Maud assured him. 'The brain is a pretty amazing thing. Neural pathways can be rebuilt.' She tried to stay upbeat. 'We're still smarter than our phones . . . for now at least.'

Maud waited patiently for his response. Porter nodded an okay, composing himself, ready to meet the strangers who were waiting inside.

'I'll be right there . . .' he called out, searching for the name. 'Joe.'

Acknowledgements

Extra special thanks to Sophie at the Sophie Hicks Agency for your untiring support during the whole process. We have to meet IRL sometime! And thanks to Leonie for using your sci-fi powers to bring this story to life along with Clem, Ruth, the entire team at Ink Road, and Maeve for the retro cover art. And to my wife and son for always coming along for the ride.

About the Author

Rohan grew up with a love of movies from his father and stories told by his mother, children's author Jamila Gavin MBE. He was an English scholar at Exeter College, Oxford University then a fellow at the American Film Institute in Los Angeles, where he began his career as a screenwriter adapting classic sci-fi novels. His first book *Knightley & Son* was one of *Kirkus'* Best Children's Books of the Year, *Sunday Times* and *Boston Globe* Book of the Week, described by the *Daily Mail* as 'a young Sherlock for our times'. It led to two sequels.

Domain was written for his son to bring the excitement of movies and tech to the page – while being a cautionary tale about screen time . . .

Thank you for choosing an Ink Road book!

For all the latest bookish news, freebies and exclusive content, sign up to the Ink Road newsletter – scan the QR code or visit Ink.to/InkRoad

Follow us on social media:

bonnierbooks.co.uk/InkRoad